NINE
AUTHENTIC
GHOST
STORIES

NINE
AUTHENTIC
GHOST
STORIES

Introduction by
KIRSTY LOGAN

BODLEIAN
LIBRARY
PUBLISHING

This edition first published in 2025 by Bodleian Library Publishing,
Broad Street, Oxford OX1 3BG
www.bodleianshop.co.uk

First published in 1886
by John Menzies & Co., Edinburgh and Glasgow
and Simpkin, Marshall & Co., London.

ISBN 978 1 85124 659 5

The Publisher would like to thank Bruce Barker-Benfield,
Graham Hogg and Ian Scott for their advice.

Publisher: Samuel Fanous
Managing Editor: Susie Foster
Editor: Janet Phillips
Picture Editor: Leanda Shrimpton
Cover design by Dot Little at the Bodleian Library
Designed and typeset by Lucy Morton of illuminati in 10.8 on 14 Dante
Printed and bound in China by C&C Offset Printing Co., Ltd.
on 120 gsm Chinese Baijin Pure Cream paper

British Library Catalogue in Publishing Data
A CIP record of this publication is available from the British Library

CONTENTS

INTRODUCTION

by Kirsty Logan

LAST WEEKEND I was invited to a party at an old house by the sea in Cornwall. It was beautiful but very remote. I was there to see my friend Marjorie; the party was for her brother, but, typical for Marjorie, she made it all about her by putting on a play and making herself the lead. All the actors had been rehearsing really hard, but they were pretty terrible—the only thing holding it together was Marjorie, who had enough charm to make up for the rest.

On the day of the party there was a wild storm: the wind howled, the rain thudded down, and the family were worried that no one would come. Everyone was feeling the stress, particularly Marjorie, who slept in and couldn't manage any breakfast. She said she felt awful and asked to skip the party. She couldn't explain why, but she had a bad feeling about it. But she knew everyone would be upset with her if she didn't do it. She spent the day resting in her room, knowing the play was really important.

The party was a success, and everyone showed up despite the storm. Right at the last minute, Marjorie appeared, wearing her floaty white costume and looking so pale. She didn't seem herself at all. She was distant and spacey, and her voice had a strange hollow tone. She chanted her lines and mimed the actions, but it was a shadow of her former performance.

Afterwards, her family went to her room and found the door locked from the inside. They forced it open—and there was Marjorie... dead! The doctor said she'd been dead for at least *five hours*. But how was that possible? They'd just seen her! And if she'd died in her sleep five hours ago... then why was she dressed for the play?

This ghostly tale might seem familiar if you've read the opening story in this collection, "Obedient unto Death." The collection was anonymously published in 1886, by John Menzies in Glasgow and Simpkin, Marshall & Co. in London, as *Nine Authentic Ghost Stories of the Century—Hitherto Unpublished*, and was almost forgotten until it was recently unearthed in the Bodleian Library—all of which seems like the beginning of a delicious ghost story in itself.

When Bodleian Library Publishing contacted me about writing this introduction, this line in the email intrigued me: "there is no named author or editor on this collection." Every one of the nine stories was initially published anonymously, and despite scholars' best efforts, to this day no author has been confirmed.

Some curators have suggested that at least one of the stories in the collection, "A Witch and Her Ghost," was written by William Robertson of Broughty Ferry (1804/8–1897), since it appears at the end of an edition of his poems. The collection does indeed lean Scottish (five of the nine stories are set in Scotland—the others being in Cornwall and Spain, with two of no specific location). Robertson was a gardener, and it's believed that he initially had his stories published in *The People's Journal*. In the late nineteenth century there were several journals, including *The People's Journal* and *The People's Friend,* which contained anonymous stories, often from amateur working-class authors. (To wrap up this conjecture, Robertson's obituary makes no mention of his being the author of ghost stories, and there is little definite proof either way; he remains a fascinating figure, with his first named publication occurring when he was aged over 90.)

The *Aberdeen Press & Journal* speculated that several of the stories could be authored by a female writer—whose name, like so many female storytellers of fairy tales, folklore and ghost tales, is lost to history. It seems that the stories are not all by a single author, as the narrators include a male Scottish gardener and a female German governess, though it's certainly possible that this is just a conceit to give the illusion of true tales.

Have you heard the true—or, I should say, *"true"*—tale of the enormous alligators in New York's sewers? Or the ghostly hitchhiker driven home on the anniversary of her death? How about Bigfoot? Mothman, the Yeti or the Loch Ness Monster?

Urban legends are a type of modern folklore, consisting of fictional stories of the ghostly, macabre and strange. Like folklore, they're shared without an author being credited, and told as if they really happened—usually not to the teller of the tale, but to their uncle, an old neighbour, or the friend-of-a-friend-of-a-friend. Traditionally they're thought of as "campfire tales," told orally at parties, sleepovers, or as gossip over a garden fence or in a supermarket queue.

CreepyPasta are what happens when urban legends go online. Shared anonymously, and often as if they're real, they proliferate on internet forums and on social media. (The name, if you're wondering, comes from a mangling of "copy–paste"—anonymously shared online stories became "copy-pasta," and horror versions of these stories became "creepy-pasta.") I've retold the story at the start of this introduction in CreepyPasta style. Some of them have a massive readership and have become part of common cultural knowledge; Slenderman, which started as a CreepyPasta, bled into the real world in tragic and unexpected ways, and is now a part of our common cultural knowledge.

Stylistically, both urban legends and CreepyPasta use a distinctive storytelling technique: they're short, told in straightforward prose, often in first-person narration, and are set in the modern day—all of which are also true of the tales in *Nine Authentic Ghost Stories*. The first story is set only a year before the collection's publication date, suggesting it was written very close to publication, or the author wanted it to appear that way to give the impression of being trendy and modern. One of the tales even states that "many of the people mentioned in this story are still alive."

So gather round the campfire (whether real or metaphorical) and delve into some ghostly tales. In reading the following stories, perhaps we can place their development on the journey from folklore passed down through generations, to publications like *Nine Authentic Ghost Stories*, to gossipy urban legends, all the way to the internet age's CreepyPasta—and to whatever sort of anonymous, viral storytelling comes next.

I

OBEDIENT
UNTO DEATH

ON A DREARY STRETCH OF MOORLAND in the south of Cornwall stands a large stone house, known as Tremorvennick, belonging, at the time of which I am writing, to the old Cornish family of Polruan. It stands alone on the moor, surrounded by curious blocks of stone, of every size and shape, which have been there from time immemorial, and which were probably the witnesses of many a Druidical ceremony in the far-off days before Christianity and civilisation were spread over the land. Not far from the house, a steep hill leads down to the sea-shore, where rugged cliffs and long stretches of seaweed-covered rocks make up a picturesque enough scene; while a short distance along the coast lies the little village of Ruan, with its fine old thirteenth-century church, its cluster of greystone cottages, with huge bushes of lemon verbena and purple fuchsia in the gardens, and its tiny quay, covered with heaps of nets and piles of fresh-caught fish.

A small out-of-the-world place is Ruan, and Tremorvennick looks little less so, standing alone among the great grey boulders, without another human habitation in sight.

Colonel Polruan, the present owner of the place, was remarkable even in Cornwall for his cordial hospitality; and, in spite of its dreary exterior, Tremorvennick was a pleasant house for its many visitors, and one where there was generally some amusement or other on the tapis.

Mrs Polruan was somewhat of an invalid, and the chief duties of entertainment usually fell on her daughter Marjory—a bright, lively girl of one-and-twenty. In the autumn of 1885, special festivities were being indulged in at Tremorvennick, to celebrate the successful entrance into the army of the eldest son, Jem Polruan. Some private theatricals were being got up, to be followed by a dance, and the house was full of guests, young and old. The play chosen was a little one-act comedy, and one of the principal actresses was Marjory Polruan; she had a good deal of natural dramatic ability, and was the life and soul of the small troupe of actors, most of whom were of the very mediocre kind one meets with on these occasions. Continual rehearsals filled up the last few days before that fixed for the representation, and plentiful occupation was provided by the many failures of several of the performers, who seemed woefully devoid of any of the "sacred fire" necessary even to amateurs. Marjory was foremost in trying to instil life and spirit into the baldness of their speeches and the woodenness of their movements; and the spectators, one and all, agreed that in her lay the chief hope of a successful performance. On the day immediately preceding that on which the festivities were to come off, the anxiety of the actors rose to such a pitch that they all declared an entire suspension of coachings and rehearsals to be necessary to their peace of mind. Accordingly, they spent the whole afternoon in the most childish amusements they could devise, ending the day by sliding down the staircase on a collection of tea-trays, until they were all in the wildest spirits, and their real or pretended nervousness, with regard to the morrow, had completely vanished. Marjory Polruan was the gayest of them all. Naturally high-spirited, she was full of almost child-like enjoyment of all and every "ploy" she came across; and when at length the evening ended, and they all separated, she went to her room full of happy anticipations of the morrow, and thinking only of the amusements it was to bring.

The next day was stormy in the extreme; the wind howled round the old house, and beat the branches of the stunted oaks, which were all that the Cornish climate could rear, against the grey boulders; while sudden showers of rain came down from time to time. When the house party met at breakfast, at a late hour in the morning, they were full of fears lest the badness of the weather should prevent the best part of their audience from appearing that evening, and many were their lamentations and suggestions. Marjory alone took no part in the conversation; she had come down very late, looking pale and wretched—a great contrast to the bright girl she had seemed yesterday. She ate nothing, and, as soon as breakfast was over, she followed her mother to her sitting-room, and astonished her by imploring to be excused from acting that night.

"Good gracious, Marjory, what can you mean?" said poor Mrs Polruan, bewildered by this sudden change. "Why do you wish not to act? You have been so keen about it ever since the idea was started."

"Yes, I know," said Marjory, looking out of the window at the distant shore, where the waves were rolling high, and dashing themselves against the rocks. "But I have a presentiment against it now, and I would give anything to be let off. *Do*, mother," she went on, looking imploringly at Mrs Polruan; "I have such a strong feeling against it—I am sure that this acting will end in misery to us all."

Mrs Polruan hesitated; she was loath to force anything on her child that was obviously contrary to her wishes; but it was probable that Marjory was only nervous and tired out. As to presentiments, they *must* be nonsense, she thought; who ever heard of anyone paying attention to a girl's "previsions"? Besides, at this short notice, who could she get to fill Marjory's place? Obviously, no one.

No; the whole play could not be allowed to fall through for these foolish fancies.

"My dearest child," she said, with a little sigh, "it is quite out of the question. I cannot allow you to throw up your part under any consideration. The whole thing would be a failure; for, you know, as it is, I depend chiefly on you to save it from coming to utter grief. The Burne girls and that irritating fellow, Arthur Trelawny, will endanger the success of the thing very much as it is by their atrocious acting; and really, Marjory," she went on, plaintively, "if *you* fail, I cannot think what is to happen. You can see for yourself how impossible it is that you should be let off. I can't think what has come over you this morning. You must be dreaming to suggest such a thing."

Marjory looked hopelessly at her mother; her attitude was one of utter despondency; and, as she turned round from the window, the light fell on her face, and showed a look of gloomy foreboding.

"Oh, mother," she said, piteously, *"won't* you let me off."

"Marjory dear, I really cannot," answered her mother. "I wish I could, as you seem so anxious, but what can I do? The play would be a complete failure. For goodness' sake, don't fail me, child—I cannot stand the worry and bother. Go and lie down, and you will feel all right when the time comes. Promise me you will act, dear.

Your father would be so vexed if the whole thing were a fiasco."

"Very well," said the girl, in a low, determined voice, "I give you my word that I will, mother. I won't fail you."

"That's my dear, little, helpful daughter," cried Mrs Polruan, as she kissed Marjory's forehead. "Why, child, how cold and wretched you look; go and rest, or you will never be fit for to-night."

"No," said Marjory, slowly; "I don't feel up to very much, and I really cannot go and talk to people all day. May I be left quite alone, mother, till the acting begins? I have a headache, and I do so want a little time to myself."

"Oh, yes," replied her mother, who, now that she had carried her point, pitied what she took to be Marjory's nervousness. "Go and keep quiet, dear, and I will send up some luncheon to your room later on."

Marjory accordingly retreated to her own room, a cosy little place, filled with pottery, books, and all the hundred-and-one knickknacks girls delight in.

"I know there is some misfortune coming," she murmured, as she threw herself into a large armchair by the fire. "I don't feel as if I *could* act tonight; but I've promised, and so I must, and will."

She lay back in a half-sleeping condition, staring dreamily at the flames as they flickered brightly, and lit up her pale face against the bright chintz of the armchair. Presently her maid appeared with some luncheon, which Marjory tried to eat, and then, feeling oppressed in the warm atmosphere of her room, and longing for a breath of fresh air, she ordered her horse, and sent word to her mother that she was going out for a ride. A few minutes later, attired in her neat, dark green habit, she came downstairs, mounted, and rode off. The strong south-westerly gale was deliciously refreshing, as it blew inland, with a faint salt smell, and the atmosphere was very different from the usual muggy warmth of a Cornish autumn. Marjory rode on, through the little village of Ruan, and down by the sea-shore, thinking of the acting which she now dreaded so heartily, and her presentiment of misfortune growing stronger and stronger every minute.

About half-past four she returned to the house, went up to her room, and, after sending for a cup of tea, dismissed her maid before she had even changed her habit, giving, at the same time, strict orders that no one was to come near her unless she rang.

"Shan't I come to dress you, or bring some dinner, nor nothink, ma'am?" said the maid, as she was leaving the room.

"No, thank you, Bryant," answered the girl, as she sat down on the rug, and stretched out her hands to the fire; "I'll have no dinner, and I shall very likely dress myself."

She got up and locked the door so as to ensure solitude, and then murmuring wearily, "I must lie down before I change my habit; I feel so faint somehow"—she threw herself on the bed.

Meantime, Mrs Polruan, relieved on the score of Marjory's unwillingness to act, and putting it all down to an attack of nervousness, sat comfortably in the drawing-room talking to some of her guests, until the time arrived that was fixed for the early dinner, previous to the theatricals. She was not surprised when Marjory failed to appear at it, and taking it for granted that she was having some food in her own room, and would prefer solitude, she did not go up to see her. Before long, carriageful after carriageful of people began to arrive, and presently the hour came at which the play was to begin. The other actors assembled one by one in the greenroom, but no Marjory appeared, until every one was ready, and the curtain about to be drawn up. Then, just as the prompter was proposing to send for her, in she came, very pale and wan, and glided silently into her place. As the play went on, Mrs Polruan, who was watching her daughter anxiously from among the audience, saw with disappointment that, far from redeeming the shortcomings of the other actors, Marjory looked tired and languid. She seemed to hold herself aloof, and to be acting as if it were a weary task she must accomplish against her will. Her voice had an odd, far-away ring in it, and was very faint and low, while she moved as if she were walking in her sleep.

Presently Mrs Polruan turned to her neighbour, a tall, elderly man, and a well-known physician in the neighbourhood, and said—

"Marjory is acting so badly to-night that I feel quite ashamed of her, Dr Pendennis."

"Miss Polruan looks extremely ill," he replied; "I have been wondering the whole time what is the matter with her. I never saw a person looking more deathlike. She ought to be in bed, and not acting."

"Good gracious! doctor," exclaimed Mrs Polruan, alarmed. "I do hope there is nothing wrong with her. I never thought she could be ill, or I would not have made her act! You don't really think so, do you?"

Dr Pendennis shook his head.

"I always told you to be careful of her," he said. "With such a weak heart as that young lady has, no precautions can be too great. She should not dance to-night, I am sure, at any rate."

"You shall see her yourself as soon as ever this wretched play is over, and tell her so," replied poor Mrs Polruan, now in a great fright lest her child should have been harmed by obeying her wishes that evening.

Presently the curtain fell, and the play was ended amidst the loud applause of the audience.

"Well," said the hero of this piece, as he turned to a pretty little girl standing near him, "I never guessed Miss Polruan would handicap us all as she did. I never saw such a change from her acting yesterday, and she looked so ill too. Where is she now?"

"There she is," replied the girl, "standing by that chair; I'm going to speak to her," but, as she approached the slender figure in white, leaning against the old oak-chair, it suddenly vanished into a room beyond. "Gone to change her dress, I suppose," said the girl, with a slight feeling of astonishment, and a little thrill of something that was almost fear came over her, when she found that there was no second door out of the room beyond, nor any trace of Marjory.

Meanwhile Mrs Polruan, accompanied by the doctor, had slipped away from among her guests the minute the curtain dropped, and had gone upstairs to her daughter's room. She knocked at the door, but heard no answer, and after a moment or two turned the handle to go in. To her surprise she found that the door was locked, and that Marjory gave no answer to her call of, "Open the door, dear child; I want to speak to you." At this instant a housemaid passed, to whom Mrs Polruan said, impatiently, "Did you see Miss Polruan come up just now, Anne?"

"No, ma'am," said the woman, and then continued, "If you please, ma'am, it was locked some time ago. I could not get in to do the room after the acting was begun, so I thought Miss Polruan had locked it herself."

"This is serious," said the doctor, and glanced at Mrs Polruan. "She must have come up, and perhaps fainted. I think I had better break the lock, if you will allow me."

"Oh, certainly, certainly," said the lady. "Poor darling, she must, as you say, have fainted."

A strong push or two soon broke in the door, and they entered the room. It was unlit, save by the light of the moon, which shone dimly through the clouds, and in at the uncurtained window. The fire was out, and for a second or two nothing was clearly visible. No one replied to Mrs Polruan's anxious "Marjory dear, where are you?" until suddenly the clouds drifted away from before the moon. A flood of pale, cold light was thrown on to the bed, and the mother sprang forward and put her hand on a dark figure that lay stretched out silent and motionless.

"Darling, darling!" she cried, "speak to me."

Then controlling herself, and turning to the doctor, she said, in a voice which shook a little with anxiety, and an unconscious foreboding of what she was about to learn,—

"You were right, doctor, she has fainted. But, merciful heaven!" she shrieked the next minute, as she attempted to raise the girl's head, "she is stone cold and stiff. I cannot move her. Doctor, doctor, what is this?"

Dr Pendennis bent down; he had just lit a candle, whose yellow light flared weirdly across the bed beside the cold moonbeam; and, after an instant's scrutiny, he said, gravely, "I hardly know how to tell it you, Mrs Polruan, but it has to be done. Your daughter must have been seized with a sudden fit of faintness, from which she never recovered. She has been dead for the last five hours at least."

"It can't be," cried the poor mother, wildly. "She was acting, we saw her not ten minutes ago! And how comes she to be in her habit? Oh, what does it all mean?"

"I cannot explain it to you," replied Dr Pendennis. "All I know is, that the facts of the case are just what I have stated to you."

"And I made her promise to act," moaned poor Mrs Polruan, "when all the time"—she stopped, and, in another second, had fallen fainting across the foot of the bed, beside the dead body of poor Marjory, whose presentiment was now sadly realised, in a way of which she herself had little dreamt.

II

A STRANGE
CONFESSION

IN APRIL OF LAST YEAR, while attending the Maternity Hospital in the capacity of a senior student, I by chance made the acquaintance of one who appeared, and who proved indeed to be a weird, strange creature. That we might be within easy reach of the hospital, another medical student and I took lodgings in the vicinity of Rotten Row. Our rooms were comfortable enough, although the passage by which we entered was dark and dirty. For a day or two our neighbours eyed us askance, wondering perhaps who we were, but ere long they were on capital terms with what they chose to call "the young howdies." Having been called out suddenly one night about ten o'clock, we found, on reaching the patient's house, that we had forgotten a drug, which, in the circumstances, it was necessary to use. Leaving my friend I hurried back to our lodgings, and was flying upstairs, taking two at a bound, when in the turn above the first floor I came violently into contact with someone who was descending. We both paused for a second until we had recovered breath, and then, knowing that the blame lay entirely with me, I said, hurriedly, "I beg your pardon, I'm sure; I hope you are not hurt." In the dim light I could hardly distinguish whether the figure was that of a man or woman, for a long, dark cloak enveloped it almost entirely. Without a word in answer to my apology, the figure, now having recovered breath, brushed me aside, and began slowly to descend. After it had moved away a step or two, I hurriedly followed, fearing that I had unwittingly given offence to one of our neighbours, with whom we were anxious to remain on good terms. By the time I had overtaken the dark figure we had reached the first landing, and stood directly beneath the gas. I quickly laid my hand on his arm—for I now saw from the black slouch hat that it was a man—and was about to repeat my excuse, but with an angry gesture my hand was shaken off, and a thin, white, shrivelled face, with hot, burning eyes, was thrust into mine, while a voice, thick with passion, and marked by a strong French accent began—"Sir—sir—you are a careless fool," and then the speaker suddenly paused as he caught a full view of my face. "Who—who—are you?" he demanded, hastily, while he grasped me tightly by the arm, and seemed as if he would read my soul with those coal-like eyes. I quickly told my name and profession, and then began to say that I was extremely sorry for the collision, but he stopped me with a wave. "I believe you," he said. "Alas, I took you for one long dead. Ah!" with a heavy sigh, as if lost in thought, "strange, strange." Then, as if recollecting himself, he said, "Adieu, sir; but I will meet you again. You will come to me tomorrow, will you not?" This with a strange, pleading tone. I promised; and then learning the name of the people with whom he lodged, I hurried up to my room, having already lost considerable time.

After that we met frequently. I found him somewhat a mystery to the other people in the building. They only spoke of him as the "queer furriner." How he made his livelihood, or where he came from, none could tell. On my visits I was able to inspect my new acquaintance more at leisure, and certainly he looked weird even in his own room. His face was thin, pale, and heavily wrinkled. He could never have been more than medium height; but now that his shoulders were rounded and his form bent he looked little more than a large-sized dwarf. The most remarkable feature was the snow-white hair which lay around the thin, smooth shaven face, and fell in long heavy masses over the bent shoulders, giving him the appearance of some Eastern wizard. He spoke with a foreign, high-bred accent, and in his every action was declared the indisputable stamp of a gentleman.

In a few weeks I had to change my lodgings to the vicinity of Gilmorehill, and, amid the worry of working for my final examination, quickly forgot my strange acquaintance of Rotten Row. One night in June, as I was reading hard for the next day, I received a brief message begging me to come at once to his lodgings. I hurried away, and found him very ill. He could not possibly live till daybreak; his lungs, which had been gradually decaying, were now almost gone.

"I have sent for you, my friend," he said, when I entered and took his hand, "for I wished you to be with me at the last. You are like—ah, so like—one I once loved, now long since dead. I have not very long to live, and I have hoped and prayed for this hour for years, every one of which has seemed to me a thousand."

I begged him not to speak any more at present, for he was becoming strangely excited, but he waved me off with his own peculiar gesture, and taking from beneath the pillow a sealed packet, he put it into my hands, bidding me not open it for twelve months. I sat with him all night, and in the early morn I closed his eyes and prepared him for the grave, whither in two days I followed the body—his only mourner. He had written an inscription, which he gave me before his death, and in a month later a tombstone bore the simple words

GUSTAVE ST. STAËL,
Ætat. 33.
Miserere Domine.

In the toil of examinations, in which I was successful, and the subsequent endeavour to lay the foundations of a practice, the packet was entirely forgotten, and only lately, in arranging some old papers, I came upon it. The year had long expired, and opening it I read with mingled emotions the strange confession, which I give in its entirety. The manuscript was in French, and I have translated it as literally as possible. On the outside of the packet was written—

A WASTED LIFE.

"How strange is love; how strange is hate! How much opposed, and yet how near and like they are! What once was love—with no reason perhaps—slowly, stealthily grows into lukewarm friendship; mere friendship gives place to dislike; this, to contempt or scorn, which finally merges into detestation and hate. Some natures—hot, passionate—are peculiarly liable to these emotions; with them, hate is as love—excessive. I, with my fiery southern soul, have experienced all the accursed pangs of these two passions. With me to hate was as to love; I could not be content with a moiety of either. My heart, my life, must be given up to the pursuit of whichever infatuated me; and so, with all my soul, I hated him I once had loved—Armaud Lavallè.

"We were natives of the same southern part of sunny France. His parents were poor, and had much difficulty in maintaining an air of respectability; while I, I was the only son of the haughty lord of the manor. When I was a mere child I had, through the carelessness of my nurse, been allowed to wander from her sight, and in the deliciousness of freedom I strayed down to the edge of the river. Stooping to pull a gaudy flower which attracted my attention, I lost my balance and fell headlong into the stream. My wild cry attracted the attention of a passer-by, who plunged into the water and saved me from an early grave, which, would to God I had been allowed to fill. That man—the man who saved my life—was the father of Armaud Lavallè.

"My father so rejoiced at the recovery of his only son, that he at once offered himself as patron to the Lavallè family. Lavallè *pére* was proud and would not be patronised, but after much persuasion he consented, as a sort of compromise, that the little Armaud, then my own age, and the youngest of a numerous family, should be given up entirely to my father, who promised to secure his advancement in the world.

"From that day Armaud and I were constantly together. I loved him as a brother. I forgot his plebeian birth, his low surroundings, his dependence for his daily bread—forgot everything save that he was very dear to me. Together we studied, together we rode, fished, and hunted. We were never separate; and when, emerging into manhood, my father proposed that I should study for a few years in the medical schools of Paris, there was no thought of separation, and Armaud and I set out together.

"Until I went to Paris I had never come in contact with any society of my own age. Armaud had been almost the only youth with whom I had ever associated; but now, the wit, the brilliancy, the wealth gathered from all parts of my native land, intoxicated—fascinated me. It was not long before I made acquaintances. I had money—plenty of it—and I spent it freely; so freely that I never lacked friends. It was then that the intimacy, almost lifelong, between Armaud and me, began slowly to cool; at least I speak for myself, for I believe he loved me truly to the end—the bitter end. Although we lived at the same hotel, and met daily in the dissecting-room, yet there was not the old converse that had bound our souls together. I indignantly repelled his gentle attempts to persuade me to give up the circle of acquaintance I had formed. I treated him in a manner which became cooler and cooler every day, and what had once been brotherly love was now swiftly changing into fierce dislike. I became reckless—yes, reckless, even among the most reckless—and more than once as I passed a group of students I noticed their cold stare, and caught the whispered word—"dissolute." At that time I took a fierce delight in the dissecting-room. The nights not spent in wild or licentious pleasure found me working there with an earnestness for which I myself could not account.

"As the session neared its close, I made what to me was a wonderful discovery—revelling, as I then was, in every kind of profligacy—that I was in love; that I loved, or thought I did, with a pure, unselfish love. The students were in the habit of visiting at the professors' houses, and frequently, while dining at the table of the Professor of Anatomy, I had met his lovely daughter, the beautiful, the angelic Marie—and she, she it was, whom I had honoured with my love.

"For a time after this discovery I improved in my habits. I withdrew myself from my dissipated companions, and sought once more the society of Armaud. He received my advances with a cordiality which was most welcome. Daily I visited, or sent anonymously some token—a flower, a book, to the lovely Marie; and at last I summoned courage and told her of my love, and offered, conscious of its acceptance, my hand. It was refused. Refused! Gently but firmly she told me that she could not love me—could not be mine—her heart was not her own, it was another's; and that other, I pleaded for his name, was—Armaud Lavallè.

"I left the house blind with rage. I could not speak— scarce think. Was it for this that I had nourished in my breast that viper? To be thus stung by that son of the gutter! To be robbed of all nearest and dearest, by one warmed at the hearth of dependence, and nursed in the lap of charity! Curse him! Ten thousand curses on him! I would yet revenge my wrongs! Thus I foamed as I hastened to the nearest café, and drank, ay, drank the accursed brandy as though it had been water, until I felt myself growing cooler and steadier. Then I sought the dissecting-room. As I made my way there, I met two or three of those youths whom Armaud had warned me against. That was enough. That they were shunned by *him* was sufficient reason that *I* should court their society. They were planning a rout for that night,—one that should surpass in debauchery any that had preceded it. "Would I join them?" they asked. "Join them? Certainly. I would be only too willing."

"In the dissecting-room we found Armaud and a few more of the steadier students hard at work. He at once saw my intoxicated condition, and looked sadly at me. That look was sufficient. It kindled ten thousand furies which had before lain dormant round my heart. I could have strangled him as he stood before me with that plaintive air. I sneered at him, and endeavoured to lead him into a quarrel, but to my bitter words he did not answer; or, if he spoke, it was with gentle tone. I became more infuriated.' He turned in silence as if to resume his work, and I—oh coward that I was!—could stand it no longer. I taunted him with his dependence, told to the wondering students, who had not dreamt of such a thing, that the aristocratic-looking Monsieur Armaud Lavallè was nought but a villager's son—a peasant, a man fitted by birth to tend swine—a man living on *my* bounty—at *my* expense. As I hurled these wild speeches at his head I expected to see him shrink and bow his head with shame. But no, he did neither. He calmly laid his scalpel down, and drawing himself up looked at me with a haughty contempt, as though *he*, not *I*, had been the injured. How I hated him as he stood looking so loftily at me! Until then I had never felt the difference in our statures. He seemed fully a foot taller than I; and as he stood with folded arms and head thrown proudly back, bringing into strong contrast the long black hair and thin handsome face, and throwing such a look of ineffable scorn from his dark, glittering eyes, I felt like a panther ready to spring upon some noble prey.

"Monsieur St. Staël,' he said, proudly, 'it is true that I am dependent upon your father's bounty, that I have been reared and educated at his expense; I have known much kindness from him in time past, and for that reason, and for the sake of our old friendship, I forgive you for what you have said to me. But from this moment I can never eat a crumb at your father's table—never use another *sou* of his.'

"He walked haughtily from the room, and, as he passed out, I laughed cruelly, heartlessly, at his words.

"The rout that night was of the most wildly exciting character. I drank deeply both of wine and brandy, but yet I could not forget my injuries—my grievous wrongs. The scene was gay, the men were reckless, but yet I could not bring myself to enjoyment. I longed to get away—anywhere—that I might be alone. The college dissecting-room alone would lend me a forgetfulness which I could not hope to find here. I rose shortly before midnight intending to seek it—professing, however, a desire to return home. My departure was loudly protested against, and I made my way out into the open air amidst much opposition. Once outside, I hurried in the direction of the college. As I turned up the avenue leading to the professors' houses, I heard two low, earnest voices a little in advance of me. One of them I fancied I recognised. I stole softly into the shade of a tree, and listened. I had not been deceived. The voice I recognised was that of Marie, and she was speaking to him—him of all men whom I loathed —Armaud Lavallè. I listened with bated breath, and heard them plight their love and promise faithfulness. He was going away on the morrow, he said, to seek for fortune, and she vowed to remain true. I gnashed my teeth as I heard him speak pityingly, lovingly of myself; and as I marked their final embrace—the last in this world—and saw him rain kisses on her cheeks, I could hear no more. I ran quickly to the bottom of the avenue and waited—waited. On he came, slowly, lost in thought. On, on. He was about to emerge from beneath the last tree, and by the light of the moon I could see his tall figure, and thin, pale face, when I rushed quickly out and confronted him. I spoke no word. I only marked his astonished look, and then

I drew from beneath my cloak my scalpel, and stabbed him to the heart. He fell without a groan, and I turned and fled to my hotel. The next morning Paris was ringing with the murder, to find a motive for which the police were completely at fault; and I, I, the dear friend and companion of the murdered man, was never suspected. I mourned deeply, and remained in close seclusion at my hotel—refusing to go abroad, refusing to be seen, refusing to be comforted. Such was the depth of my grief!

"At the end of a week I grew tired of the unaccustomed quiet. I had consumed a large amount of brandy in the interval—not to deaden the gnawing of conscience, for I felt no pang, I gloried in the deed—I had revenged myself—but because I had grown to love it. At midnight, on the sixth day after the murder, I sallied forth from the hotel towards the dissecting-room. My head was hot, burning, for I had drunk almost a bottle of brandy during the day, and now carried a large flask filled to the brim. The moon was shining bright, but I did not care for beauty then; I was thinking, gloating on my revenge. I strolled leisurely, and in a short time reached the dissecting-room. I applied my key, and soon stood in the chamber of the dead. What a strange, weird fascination that room, that charnel-house had for me! Around were strewn heads, arms, skulls, bones, decaying and putrid flesh—some covered, some uncovered, just as the students chanced to have been using them the previous day; and here and there a skeleton was suspended from the roof, or fastened to the wall. Upon this ghastly scene, this dread display of frail humanity, the moon threw a pale, unearthly light, which would have frozen the blood around the stoutest, manliest heart, and chilled to death the cruellest bravado; but for me it possessed an attraction at that moment which no other scene could wield.

"I took a long draught at my flask, and turned to look for a candle. There were none. The janitor had evidently omitted to provide a supply, and it was now too late to buy them in the city. Never mind. The moon was bright, and sufficient light streamed through the iron-barred window to allow me to work. I threw off my cloak and hat, and advanced to one of the long tables whereon lay a new subject wrapped in a white sheet. I took another draught at my flask, draining it this time. I felt the liquor coursing through my veins, tingling at my finger points, surging round my brain and heart, and then I swore I was a new man. I took up my scalpel, and threw off the sheet which enfolded the corpse, and looked with a start, a wild demoniac gladness, upon the face of him, my foe, my enemy Armaud Lavallè. At first I could not believe my eyes. Could it really be he? How came he in such a place? I looked for the wound in the heart. It was there! Ah! I understood it now. No one had come forward to claim him at the Morgue, and his dead body had fallen into the possession of the authorities of the medical school. I remembered that I had never written home. His parents could not know yet of his death, and they would never know from me.

"As I gazed upon the dead body, all the old hate, the detestation, the sense of injury, of wrong, swept over me. I pictured to myself the scene in this same room a week ago—his contemptuous look, his pitying words, his proud, noble bearing. Again I saw the parting in the avenue, heard once more the kisses rained upon the willing cheeks, heard the plighted troth, heard myself spoken of with love, heard—but I could bear it no longer. I was mad—mad with hate. I had not been half revenged. I would tear his heart from the roots, and press it beneath my feet. In a frenzy I seized my scalpel, dug it deep into the heart, and laughed in the dead man's face. As I looked and laughed, I felt the blood slowly freezing in my veins. The eyes of him I had thought dead—of him at whose heart I was tugging with my knife—opened, and fixed on me a glassy stare, which transfixed me with fear and horror. My laugh died away in a wild, frenzied shriek. My hair seemed to stand upright, and my blood to turn to ice. As I gazed, the body rose—with my knife still in its heart—rose, still holding me spellbound with that same glassy look, and, stretching out its arms, clutched with its long, gaunt fingers my throat. In vain I struggled to free myself. The fingers tightened. I endeavoured to unlock them. It was vain! My head was growing dizzy, but still I struggled—struggled with the energy of despair. I could not speak. I felt my face growing black, felt the blood rushing to my brain, and then with one last supreme effort I strove to free myself. It was useless! The skinny, clammy fingers tightened more and more. I could not breathe. I was dying, dying, choking. O God! help me, pardon me!

"I must have lain for many hours. When I opened my eyes again, it was in answer to restoratives which were being applied by one of the professors and several students. I looked wildly around. The corpse was gone. I pointed to the empty table. 'Where, where?' I asked. The professor shook his head. He could not understand; but when one of the students stooped and lifted the empty brandy flask, he seemed to comprehend. He looked pityingly at me as he said, 'You will kill yourself, St. Staël.' After a while I recovered sufficiently to rise, and then I asked what had been done with the subject. The professor explained that it had been brought on the previous evening after the students had left; but in the morning, when it was discovered whose body it was, it had been removed at once, and was then awaiting burial. They attributed my insensibility partly to the brandy I had drunk and partly to the shock at finding my friend in such a place. They knew nothing of the awful struggle. I was taken to my hotel in a carriage, and on gaining my room and looking into the mirror, what there did I see? O God! Not the face I had looked at yesterday. That pale, shrivelled face could not be mine! That hair blanched white as snow with the terrors of a single hour was not the glossy black I had combed with such care the night before! And my throat—around it were the pale, faint marks of fingers—marks which will remain till my dying day. Within an hour I left Paris—France; left the home of my birth, my fatherland; left my aged sire, my mother, all, everyone—to become a wanderer, an outcast, looking, ever looking for that nepenthe, those waters of Lethe—forgetfulness. Though my hair is white and my brow furrowed, I am not an old man. But this careworn, hunted look, these trembling hands, will never pass away. For in the silent midnight watches I see again that glassy stare; I see again the corpse arise; I feel again the tightening fingers round my throat; I struggle, I shriek for help, but all in vain. I am in the hands of a ruthless avenger; a cruel, relentless pursuer—the *memory* of the murdered Armaud Lavallè!"

A WITCH AND
HER GHOST

ABOUT FORTY-SIX YEARS AGO I was employed as gardener to a gentleman in the Highlands of Perthshire, where the incidents occurred which I am about to relate.

Being a single man, I occupied a small room, distant fully a quarter of a mile from my work, and where, I might say, I acted as "guide, philosopher, and friend" to myself.

A woman, to all appearance very old, was my next-door neighbour. She had a wild and weird-like look, and the expression of her eyes was simply appalling. A thin partition separated her apartment from mine, and I could hear her spinning-wheel going every Sunday, herself at the same time humming a mournful Gaelic air, as an accompaniment to the *birr* of her wheel.

By the natives all round she was regarded with superstitious dread, and the boldest would not venture to incur her displeasure. So great was the awe she inspired that she could enter houses and, unchallenged, take from press or cupboard bread, butter, or cheese, whilst none of the cowed inmates would dare to interfere.

It seemed to be an understood thing among the natives that, should anyone be unfortunate enough, by any means whatever, to incur her displeasure, a terrible calamity would soon overtake them.

The reader will perhaps be surprised when I state that I was rash enough to somewhat rudely dispute her right to pillage my press, seeing I am alive, and unscathed by devilry or witchcraft of any kind. I am impelled, however, to confess, that had I not been a man of more than ordinary nerve, I would most assuredly have been frightened out of my wits by this same witch, *six years after she was dead and buried.*

The startling statement I have now made, and the incidents that follow, I solemnly declare were witnessed by me.

Before proceeding further with my story I wish to state that I am very far from being superstitious, and I am equally free from slavish fears, and have, since I arrived at manhood, been an independent and, I may add, a fearless thinker. My courage, however, was put to a test that

> Might have strewed the snows of age
> On youth's auburn ringlets,
> or blighted Beauty's rosy cheek for ever.

How I had nerve sufficient to brave the appalling sight I was doomed to witness I have never been able to satisfy myself, and it remains an unexplained puzzle to me to this day.

Gardeners during winter, when the weather is too cold and stormy for work out-of-doors, generally take to the house, and employ themselves in making baskets to carry fruit or vegetables to the great man's house.

On a very cold and tempestuous day I sat in my apartment engaged at basket-making, and listening to the spinning-wheel, and the low, wailing notes of the so-called witch's Gaelic air. By-and-by the wheel, and the sad music that accompanied it, ceased, and in less than five minutes my door was opened, and in entered the old hag for the first time, "withered, wild, and ragged in her attire." I was honoured with a glance that seemed to me absolutely infernal in its expression, and hideous in its wrinkled deformity. From what I had heard of her I expected my press would be laid under contribution; and so it was, for, with a look of resolute determination, thither she went, and at once commenced to pillage its contents. Not relishing such familiarity, I rose and stepped towards her, and laying my hands on her shoulders, wheeled her round and pushed her out, barring the door behind her. Just as the door closed, she turned round and gave vent to a shriek so frightful as to ring in my ears like a howl from the damned.

Next day, in conversation with the grieve, I told him what I had done, seeming, at the same time, to treat the affair lightly.

He shook his head, and said, "Man, I would not have done what you say for fifty pounds!"

I replied, "I would do it again for far less," adding, "I am not afraid of witches."

"You will break your neck, or leg, or be drowned some of these days," he replied; adding, as he moved off, "Mind what I say!"

When six months had nearly expired, the old lady died and was buried, the neighbours wondering all the while why I had escaped unharmed from the vengeance of this terrible witch. I was careful to take a note of the year and day of the month on which she was buried; this I jotted down on the flyleaf of a favourite book.

Before proceeding further with my story, I wish it to be distinctly understood that I have no intention to magnify my own courage and resolute bearing under the frightful ordeal I was doomed to encounter. I can only say that I was sustained in a mysterious way beyond my comprehension. Let me explain how I felt. I felt my muscles tighten, and a strength and firmness of body and limb, as if I had been a man of iron. In short, I stood boldly convinced that my right of way on earth was as good as any ghost's could be, and it is questionable whether a psychologist could give a better reason. Why this strange old creature should always regard me with a look of intense hatred, which she did every time she met me, I cannot explain; at all events, I would have rendered her all the kindness in my power, had not her deportment towards me made that impossible.

Some four or five months after her death I removed to a situation in Forfarshire, a distance from my Highland abode of about thirty-five miles as the crow flies. *It was here I met the ghost of the witch*—a pretty long distance from the spot where her bones were mingling with the clods of the valley. I had been married, and had settled down in my new abode for some years, when I got leave of absence for two or three days to go and see a friend who had returned from abroad in bad health. I was on my return home when I met the witch, enveloped in horrors—a veritable embodiment of all imagination can conceive of the terrible in the world unseen.

It was late in the day when I started on my journey, and, being winter, darkness soon set in, but in other respects it was a pleasant night for the season. Between one and two o'clock in the morning I had reached within a mile or so of my home, and, having nothing to hurry me, was walking leisurely along. On my right hand was a lea-field, which terminated at a thick belt of young fir-trees about 150 yards in advance of where I was walking. At that moment I happened to look forward to the dreary-looking line of trees, and then it was I saw a dark-looking, ill-defined figure move out on the lea about fifteen feet or thereby from the road, and approaching rapidly in a straight line down the field. Owing to the darkness, I should not have seen the figure till it came nearer; but, at all events, I did see it the moment it emerged on the field. When opposite me, I saw it kneel in a halo of intense light, which shot out tremulous rays into the darkness, with a low spluttering noise, in all directions. My astonishment knew no bounds the moment I discovered that the figure kneeling before me was the *witch*, grasping her staff with her skinny hands, and holding it upright in front of her. I recognised every patch on her tattered cloak, her staff, the terrible expression of her eyes, more frightful now than ever; and I could see her toothless gums when she opened her thin lips, from which proceeded horrid mutterings, seemingly devilish in their import.

"If this is not a ghost, there never was one," I thought to myself.

Horrors upon horrors! looking into her eyes, which blazed like two furnaces, I could see in their far depths *a tiny image of myself*, standing, as it were, in a sea of flame. So intensely awful was the sight that it made me instinctively utter, "Merciful God, support and protect me at this moment." A sound like the flap of a bird's wing made me look up, and there I saw, above the kneeling figure, a ring of a lurid red colour, about five feet in diameter, and stationary. So threatening in their expression were the features of the apparition, that every moment I expected it would spring at me. I was about to move away, when I observed the ring slowly descending, whilst the figure, at the same time, rose slowly, as if to meet it; and when the head and shoulders of this frightful phantom rose above the ring and stood at its centre, the spectacle was appalling in a terrible degree. Suddenly the ring again began to descend, the wild glaring eyes all the while fixed on me, fierce and undefinable in their hate. No sooner had the ring reached the ground than the fiend-like features relaxed, the eyes grew dimmer, the ring seemed to sink into the earth, the halo of light vanished, and a dark form stood a few moments in gloomy stillness, then slowly melted into the shades of night.

In passing the wood from which I first noticed my unearthly visitor emerge, I felt a shock rattle through my brain like a shower of icicles, and on raising my hand to my head I found my hair drenched with a cold, clammy sweat, and a momentary giddiness came over me, but soon passed away. On my return home I looked up the book in which I had noted the witch's death, and found, curiously enough, that it was exactly six years since the witch died and was buried. Though it is now well-nigh fifty years since the occurrence of the event which I have related in my story, I have still a most vivid recollection of all the incidents of which, improbable as it may seem, I was an unharmed eye-witness.

IV

MY GREAT-GREAT-
GRANDMOTHER'S
GHOST

M Y Dear Harold—I was in town to-day and saw your Aunt Helen, who informed me that you were coming to Edinburgh to attend college, and that she was looking for lodgings for you. I write to propose that you should take up your abode with us. There is plenty of room, our family being small, as you know. We are not more than ten miles from town, and a very short way from the station. We live very quietly, so that you would not be disturbed at your studies. So, if you care to accept this proposal, a most cordial welcome awaits you from your aunt and myself.

In haste.—I am, your affectionate Uncle,

John P. Gilmour

Such was the letter I received, and I did not hesitate to accept the kind invitation it contained.

A few weeks later I left home, and, after a long and wearisome journey, reached Cherriton just about night-fall.

It was a good, solid, but uninteresting-looking house, surrounded by fine old trees, which may have been the cause of its frowning and gloomy appearance in the dim light of the stars.

After a hearty welcome and a substantial meal we sat for a while around the fire, talking about family affairs and my future life.

"Well, Harold, as you must be tired after your journey, I'll show you your room," said my aunt.

I followed her into the hall, where we turned to the right, and entered a passage at the back of the dining-room. At the end of the passage my aunt opened a door, and ushered me into a room which might have appeared somewhat gloomy, but for the cheerful warmth of a bright fire.

"I thought this room would be the quietest in the house. It is quite away from the noise of the kitchen, and, though it is next to the dining-room, these old walls are so thick and well deafened that I think you will not be disturbed by noise from us there. In this little room adjoining you can keep your books and do your writing."

I thanked her for her kind thoughtfulness.

"I hope you will be comfortable," she continued. "I think it is a pleasant room, although it has not been used for years. Now, good-night; we breakfast at half-past eight."

She closed the door, and I was left to examine my new abode.

The bedroom was low-roofed, and had only one window, which looked to the front. The writing-room of which my aunt had spoken was small, and it, too, had but one window, looking into the garden. It was furnished with a writing-table, a chair, and a few book-shelves. On one wall hung a queer old picture without a frame. It was the portrait of a lady, attired in the short waist and high mob cap worn a hundred and fifty years ago; but the face had a sad, joyless expression, which impressed me unpleasantly. I took it to be the portrait of an ancestress, and resolved to ask my uncle who she was.

Tired with the journey, and the unusual events of the day, I soon dropped asleep; but was suddenly awakened by hearing wheels on the gravel beside my window.

I had no recollection of either my aunt or uncle having said that visitors were expected; but they might have forgotten to mention it, or the arrival might be that of an unexpected guest. At all events, I was too wearied to trouble myself about the matter, and, without curiosity, I went to sleep.

Fate seemed to have destined that my rest was not to be undisturbed; for I woke with a start, hearing, as I fancied, the writing-room door shut.

I got up, and struck a light, but nothing was to be seen. Everything was as I had left it an hour-and-a-half ago; for on looking at my watch I found the hour to be half-past twelve. I had scarcely lain down again when I heard the rattle of wheels on the gravel, louder and more distinct than formerly.

"Oh!" thought I, "that's the carriage going away, and what I heard was the carriage-door shutting. All right, I hope I shall sleep now."

At breakfast next morning, seeing no appearance of other guests, I said—

"By-the-bye, had you visitors last night?"

"Visitors!" they all exclaimed, in astonishment. "We had no visitor but yourself."

"What put visitors in your head, Harold?" asked my aunt.

"I thought I heard wheels about half-past twelve, and a second time soon after."

"I think you must have imagined it," said my aunt.

"I don't think so, but it may have been a train or something. By-the-bye, Uncle John, whose portrait is that which hangs in the writing-room adjoining my bedroom?"

"Oh, that, Harold, is your great-great-grandmother; and a gruesome-looking dame she is."

"She is not prepossessing," I said.

On the afternoon of that day, while my Cousin Lucy and I were sitting in the dining-room I heard once more the sound of wheels.

"Who is this coming?" I said, going to the window. I looked out, but to my surprise there was no one. Lucy flushed crimson.

"It is nothing," she said, trying to look unconcerned. "There are so many mines in this neighbourhood that one cannot account for the strange sounds that one hears."

"Is Cherriton undermined?" I asked.

"Oh, no."

She presently asked some trivial questions, plainly showing that on the subject of "sounds" she did not desire to prolong the conversation. This roused my curiosity, but I made no further remark.

That night I sat in my bedroom reading, and had almost forgotten the disturbance of the previous night, when, just as the clock in the hall struck half-past twelve, I heard the mysterious noise on the gravel outside, so long and so loud that I jumped off my seat and rushed to the window to see—nothing.

When I turned to resume my seat I was greatly surprised to see the writing-room door wide open, although I knew that not a minute ago it was shut. I seated myself directly opposite the writing-room door, and waited to see the issue of this strange phenomenon. Nothing further, however, occurred, and I entered the room in order to fasten the window, which I had observed to be unfastened. On coming out, I suddenly felt myself enveloped in a dark shadow, which seemed to come between me and the lamp on the table. With a strange feeling of something approaching fear I closed the door with a bang, and went to bed. I could read no more that night, and only after some time did I fall asleep.

Daylight sometimes tends to efface delusions of the night, and in the morning I laughed at myself for giving way to such timorous fancies. Resolving to make no allusion to what I thought I had seen and heard, I joined my uncle's family at breakfast.

"When is your first post, Uncle John?" I said. "There ought to be a letter from home this morning."

"He is not very punctual, our post," said Lucy; "there are too many houses of refreshment on the way."

"Lucy! Lucy!"

"Oh, here he comes," I exclaimed, as I heard the sound of wheels on the gravel.

My uncle and aunt exchanged glances, and smiled almost pathetically.

"John M'Turk is a walking post," said Lucy.

"It is not quite *his* time yet; you will likely meet him on your way to the station. And, by the way, it is time you were off, Master Harold, if you don't mean to miss the train."

"You will often hear that noise, Harold," remarked my uncle, with a smile. "Don't mind it. We fancy it is caused by some reverberation, owing to the coal mines in the district. We have heard it for years, but much more frequently of late."

"More frequently of late," added my aunt, gently. "It is not to be accounted for, so off you go," said Lucy, in her brisk manner.

All through the day thoughts of the strange occurrence of the previous night haunted me. At one moment I made up my mind that there must be something uncanny at Cherriton; at another, that imagination alone was to blame for whatever appeared unusual, because, in the prosaic nineteenth century, there are neither ghosts nor apparitions. I determined, however, to watch.

When I went to my room that night I put on more coal, opened the writing-room door, and sat down to read by the side of the fire. From my chair I could see through the open door the greater part of the interior of the little writing-room. I sat reading for a while, interested in my book, and not thinking of anything beyond. Rising to stir the fire, I happened to glance towards the writing-room door, and saw, right in the doorway, a great black shadow, as of a stout man, muffled in a cloak. Like one turned to stone I stood staring at it, nor could I take my eyes off the shape, which advanced into the room a few paces, then vanished. The same eerie feeling crept over me, as of the proximity of death. Nerving myself, I took up the lamp, entered the mysterious cabinet, and made a minute search. It was in vain; I could find no explanation; all remained still and undisturbed.

I passed a somewhat restless night; and as I had to start early in the morning I left without seeing any of the family.

All through the day, while in the railway carriage, while walking on the street, while sitting in the class-room, I kept longing to get back to my room; but finally resolved to say nothing about what I had seen until I had again attempted to fathom the mystery. Eager and curious I was; but, at the same time, I felt I could not shake off an unnameable fear—of what I knew not.

The writing-room had a sort of fascination for me. It was there the form dwelt, if it had really any existence. So, after I had said good-night and gone to my room—which I did earlier than usual, on the plea of having work to do—I placed the lamp behind me, in order that its full glare should fall on the spot where the "thing" had stood the night before. Opening the door about one-half I sat down once more to wait the result.

I thought of what I should say, should the shape appear again, when, happening to look up—oh, horror, what a sight met my eye! A woman's pale, emaciated face, looking at me from the open door. Where had I seen that face? Yes, I had seen it; yet no—I could not call it to remembrance. All this flitted across my brain in an instant. So taken by surprise was I that speech and power of collected utterance fled. The book in my hand fell, and the face was gone. My courage and my resolve to clear the matter up for myself failed me, and I got up to see my uncle, who might still be in the study. On opening the door I suddenly found myself in the arms of the housemaid.

"My good woman, what's the matter," I exclaimed, trying to disengage myself. At that moment my uncle opened his door.

"What's all this about," cried he. "Nancy, what *is* the matter?"

"Oh, sir, oh dear, oh dear, come qu-i-ckly; Agnes is —deein'. Oh me," here the poor woman fairly gasped for breath. We all rushed to the kitchen, and found Agnes, the cook, half-lying, half-sitting, on the floor, supported by Andrew, the gardener, who sat helpless-looking, with open mouth, and eyes staring from their sockets.

"She's comin' tae," he said, in a loud whisper, as we entered.

Agnes seemed to have fainted; but after my aunt had administered a little wine, the patient was soon so far recovered as to explain what had happened.

Let me give it in her own words.

"Oh, mem, a' was gaw'n round tae the gairden tae fetch in the towels, and jist when I was passin' the window o' the wee room aff Maister Harold's room, wha s'ould a' see but a great muckle man." (Here my

53

uncle interrupted: "A man, Agnes! Dear me, the sight of a man does not generally affect cooks in that way.") "He was leanin' agin it, an' he vanished afore ma vera e'en; ay, mem, while I was lookin' at him. It was nae man, it was a speerit; an' I'll no stay here another nicht after the morning. The Lord preserve us a' frae sic a fricht!"

"And what was he like, Agnes?" asked my uncle, laughing!" Anything like Andrew, there?"

"Preserve us a'! no the least like Andrew," ejaculated Agnes; "a great muckle man, row'd in a cloak or something. Na, na! No like Andrew ava!"

In the dining-room I described to them what I had seen. My uncle and aunt, though apparently annoyed, did not seem so much surprised as I would have expected. Lucy seemed rather startled.

"That's the mystery explained at last, Kate," said he, turning to my aunt. "You," he said, turning to me, "have explained for us a mystery which *we* never could explain. My father would not allow that room to be used as a bedroom, but would never give a reason. 'Use it as a day-nursery if you like, or a sitting-room, but nothing else,' he said. Nothing would induce him to sit in it either, but we thought that it was just nervousness; he was a very nervous man. When you were coming we decided to give you the room. I have slept in it myself and never saw anything."

"I suppose you will be afraid to sleep there now?" said Lucy, banteringly.

"Oh," I said, "it won't make any difference sleeping there, ghosts are harmless sort of beings, or 'speerits,' as cook would say, though rather startling neighbours; and to one who had never encountered anything of the kind I must say that to see a pale lady looking at you *is* rather alarming."

"Dear me" (in the same strain as her father had spoken to the cook), "the sight of a lady doesn't generally alarm a young man," quoth Lucy.

The following day we were having a conference in the haunted chamber. My uncle suddenly turned and opened the writing-room door. My eye caught the picture of my great-great-grandmother's portrait. "Oh, that's the face," I said, half to myself.

"What's the face; what do you mean?" cried my uncle.

"Oh, that's the face of the lady I saw last night."

"Most extraordinary," ejaculated he; "I must have this investigated."

Accordingly, a few days later, they began to dismantle the two rooms.

One morning, or rather forenoon, a crash was heard. It resounded through and shook the whole house.

All rushed to the mysterious rooms from whence it seemed to originate.

In the bedroom nothing was to be seen, but in the

little room there lay the old picture on the floor. It had in its fall struck on something sharp, and there it lay with a great hole torn across it.

Instead of being hung, the picture had been fixed on the wall. My uncle said he remembered it having a frame, but that it fell off and broke to pieces, and was never restored. When last the room had been papered it was found that it was impossible to take the picture down without injuring it, so they had just papered round it. Lucy stood upon a chair to examine the old paper behind the picture. Imagine our surprise when her hand went right through the wall, as we supposed. Lucy jumped down as if she had been shot. My uncle stood up and tore away the paper, when a small crevice was seen in the wall about four or five inches square. From this he drew a little box: it contained only a roll of musty old manuscript.

How shall I describe our astonishment?

"I suppose this will clear up the mystery connected with this room," said my uncle, and he forthwith proceeded to read it. He had not read much when his face became very grave.

"Oh," he said, "this is a serious affair! I shall be with you in a short time."

He and aunt went to the library and shut the door, leaving Lucy and me to exercise patience to the best of our ability. About an hour after they both appeared looking very subdued.

"Now, papa," cried Lucy, "do tell us what is in that musty old thing? I am dying to know."

"Do you know anything of the family history?" my uncle asked of me.

"Not much," I replied.

"Well, you know," said he, "that my great-grandfather and his brother were left orphans. My great-grandfather was the younger of the two, but he was married first, and brought his bride to this house. About a year after the marriage his elder brother died, and he came into this property, being the only heir. Now, you may read that aloud for Lucy's and your own edification."

I shall not give the full contents of the manuscript, but only a few extracts.

"This confession of my crime is written by me, Jane Syme Gilmour. I married in 1735 Arthur Gilmour. He brought me here to live in his brother's house. My brother-in-law was very kind to me. Would to God he had not been so!... He kept urging my husband to look for something whereby to gain a living, saying, what was perfectly true, that if he (my brother-in-law) thought of marrying, of course he would have to live elsewhere.

At last they quarrelled—I of course siding with my husband... Together we laid a dark plot to kill my brother-in-law by slow poison; then, we being rid of him, would succeed to the property and money.... Though a doctor was in attendance almost every day we were never found out, and in about three months from the time of the quarrel, all was over. Alas, no! It was never over for me. I have been in torment ever since, and if it had not been for my child I would have put an end to my life. My husband and I never agreed afterwards. He grew morose, and took no interest in anything. How we have been punished for our crime. If ever wretch repented of a crime, I have repented over mine. That wretch, indeed, am I. My husband died a few years after the perpetration of the crime. On his deathbed he besought me, for the peace of his soul, to write out this confession... Before his death he used to wander up and down in the garden for hours at a time. Sometimes he would come indoors, and walk up and down between the room where his brother died, and the little room adjoining.... I hid this in the secret way which has been adopted, so that a considerable time might pass before it should be discovered."

With this the manuscript ended, and here may end my story. But I shall add that the furniture was put back, and that I used these rooms all the time of my sojourn with my uncle. I never had another visitor from the other world.

Agnes made up her mind to stay another night. Another night turned into several years, and Agnes never saw another "speerit."

NOTE—The main facts of this story are authentic, and have excited a good deal of attention in the household in which they took place very recently.

V

A SPANISH
GHOST STORY

I T IS NOW ABOUT TWENTY YEARS since I took honours in the examination qualifying me to teach in Höhere Töchterschulen. A week or two after the examination the Principal of the College called, asking me whether I should care to take a situation in Spain. He told me he had two Spanish boarders, Garcia by name, and that the mother of these boys had asked him to send her a governess for her daughters. The duties were light, and the salary good. I asked him whether he knew Mrs Garcia?

"Personally, not at all," he answered; "but I know that she is wealthy, and of good position."

I should have liked to know more about her than that, but the situation was too good to be refused, so I said I would go, and three weeks after I found myself in Seville.

Mrs Garcia received me very kindly, and introduced to me my pupils—Carmen, aged thirteen, and Concepcion, aged ten. After supper, she herself showed me my rooms, which were on the first floor, close to her own. The sitting-room opened off the bedroom, not off the corridor, so that it could only be reached by going through the bedroom. It had a door opening on a staircase, but Mrs Garcia said that door was of no use, as the staircase was unused, and the door at the foot of it locked. It was an odd arrangement altogether; the staircase went no further than the first floor, and communicated only with two rooms—my sitting-room, and a room opposite, which Mrs Garcia said was a lumber room, and which was locked. This sitting-room was really a splendid room; it had a marble floor, and was upholstered in red silk, with gold fringe. I wondered that so handsome a room should have been given up to me.

I was very comfortable with the Garcias, though I disliked two members of the household—an old witch of a servant, who had been Mrs Garcia's nurse, and the father confessor. The old witch used to cross herself whenever she saw me, and mutter something which may have been a prayer for my conversion, but which sounded more like a curse. Father Avila, on the other hand, was very polite; in fact, I had an uncomfortable feeling that if I gave him any encouragement he would be too polite. I saw him constantly, for he passed at least half of every day at the Garcias.

One night I was awakened by the sound of footsteps in my sitting-room. I thought something was the matter, and my help was wanted, so I rose, lit my candle, and opened the door between the rooms. There was nobody there. I tried the door to the staircase; it was locked and the key was inside. I began to think I must have been mistaken. Certainly if Mrs Garcia wanted me she would never have thought of going down to the courtyard, opening the door of the disused staircase, and coming to my sitting-room. She would simply have crossed the corridor from her bedroom to mine. Besides, the door was locked. I must have been mistaken. Accordingly I went back to bed.

A night or two after this I had gone to bed later than usual, and, just as I was putting out my light, I heard someone moving about in the sitting-room. A chair was pushed back from the table, and someone began to walk up and down the room. This time there could be no mistake. I distinctly heard the footsteps on the marble. Again I rose and opened the door. No one was to be seen. There was no place in the room where one could hide, and no way of getting out of the room except down the staircase or through my bedroom. The staircase door was locked, and no one could have got into my bedroom without passing me. I could not understand it. I heard the same noises now and then for the next fortnight, and could find no explanation of them. At last I resolved to speak to Mrs Garcia.

Next morning at breakfast I told my story, and Carmen exclaimed, "It is Papa!" and began to talk quickly in

Spanish. We always spoke French at meals, as Mrs Garcia knew no German, and I knew only a few sentences of Spanish which I had picked up since I came to Seville. Most of what Carmen said was quite unintelligible to me, but I could make out that I was not the first person who had heard these noises, and that the children believed their father's ghost haunted that room.

After breakfast Mrs Garcia came to me and said that she would like to get Father Avila to say certain prayers in my sitting-room. I said, "First tell me what it is you wish to exorcise." She answered, "My husband died suddenly in that room, without having received the last rites of the church, and I believe that his soul cannot rest." I felt that if I had to choose between Father Avila and the ghost, I decidedly preferred the ghost; but I could scarcely say so to Mrs Garcia, so I said nothing, and Father Avila recited his prayers.

All in vain. The noises continued. I believed it was some trick of the servants—possibly the old witch wanted to get rid of the heretic—and was resolved to catch the offender. I was becoming quite worn out by having my sleep so often broken, and Carmen, too, began to be troublesome. When told to do anything she disliked she would appeal to her mother; and if Mrs Garcia took my part Carmen would say, "If you don't let me do as I wish, I'll tell. I can tell, you know I saw," and thereupon Mrs Garcia would yield.

At last I thought of a plan. A great bell hung in the courtyard to be rung in case of fire. From the window of my room I could easily reach the bell-rope. I told Mrs Garcia that next time I heard the noises I would ring this bell and summon the household, and we would have the whole place searched. Mrs Garcia agreed. Two or three nights after, I heard the noises again. This time the footsteps came up to my bedroom door, and the handle of the door turned. I opened the door quickly—no one there—then I rushed to the window, and pulled the bell-rope with all my might. The whole household assembled. We began by examining the staircase. No one was there, and the door was locked and fastened in the inside with a strong bolt. Then the lumber-room was opened and thoroughly searched, but we found no one. The lumber-room had no door but the one opening from the staircase. At last we gave up the search, and went back to bed.

Next day was a festa, and we had a holiday. The German Consul's wife invited me to accompany her to the opera. I had brought letters of introduction to a good many Germans, and many of them had invited me to their houses; but Mrs Garcia, though she never objected in words to my making friends, always wanted me to go somewhere with her, so that I had never been able to accept these invitations. To-day, however, I insisted on going to the opera, saying that I had been much agitated the night before, and that I must have some distraction; and Mrs Garcia, after many objections, consented.

There was another lady at the Consul's, a Mrs Schröter, who had been in Seville for many years. She seemed to take rather a fancy to me, for she would talk to no one else, and after telling me all about her affairs, she proceeded to ask about mine.

"And you are a governess, Fraulein Schaller? May I ask in what family?"

"In Mrs Garcia's," answered I.

"What!" exclaimed the old lady. "In Mrs Garcia's? Widow of Pedro Garcia?"

"Yes," said I.

"But do you not know then, that you are in the house of a Lucrezia Borgia? Have you not heard her story?"

"I have heard no story about her," said I.

So she told me the story, and a horrible one it was. Mrs Garcia had been the wife of Pedro Garcia, the senior partner in the firm of Garcia Brothers. They did not get on well together, and Mr Garcia ended by becoming jealous of his own brother Carlos. One day Pedro and his wife had an unusually violent quarrel, and Pedro left the house in a rage. On his return his wife met him all smiles and sweetness, and brought him coffee with her own hands. An hour or two later, his valet going into his sitting-room found him seated at the table, his head resting on his arms. Something in his master's attitude struck the man as peculiar; he spoke, got no answer; touched him—he was stiff and nearly cold. The valet called the servants and ran for a doctor. When the doctor came, he said Mr Garcia had been dead for some time, and asked what he had eaten last. The cook said "coffee," and pointed to the cup still on the table. "Let me see that," said the doctor, going toward the table. The old nurse jumped up, as though to hand him the cup, but managed to upset both cup and saucer, and break them. The matter was hushed up—people said by dint of bribery—and after a decent interval the widow married Carlos Garcia. The marriage had only lasted about a year, when Carlos Garcia went mad. He accused himself of having caused his brother's death, and declared he both heard and saw the dead man continually. Six months afterwards he died. Mrs Garcia was not well received by the Seville ladies, and was said to find her life very dull, though she consoled herself with the society of Father Avila, who had the reputation of being the worst priest in Seville.

Next day I gave Mrs Garcia a quarter's notice. She was not well pleased, and tried to persuade me to stay, but I would not. A week or two after, I went up to the music-room one evening to practise. I had to pass along a dimly-lit corridor, with recesses here and there. Suddenly a man rose from one of these recesses, and threw his arm round me, exclaiming, "My dearest, my Visitacion!"

It was Father Avila. Mrs Garcia's name was Visitation. I screamed, and tried to free myself. The moment Father Avila saw who I was he let me go, and I rushed off to my own room. I had been in a nervous state since I had heard Mrs Garcia's story, and the fright I had got made me really ill. I went to bed, and after some time fell asleep. Some time later I awoke, to find my door open; a light in the passage showed me Father Avila and the old nurse standing in the doorway, and Mrs Garcia at the foot of my bed, with a cup in her hand. I sat up in bed, and asked, "What is the matter?" Mrs Garcia started, and the contents of the cup were spilt on the bed. Instantly the light went out, and a moment after I heard the door shut. I struck a light—there was no one in the room. I lay awake trembling for a long time, but at last fell asleep again. In the morning I tried to persuade myself it was fancy, and to convince myself I examined the bed-coverings, where the cup had been spilled, to see whether there was a stain. I found them burned into holes. Having dressed as quickly as possible, I went to the house of the German Consul, telling him what I had seen, and begging his assistance. He welcomed me warmly; and after much difficulty, and not without the use of threats of what might be revealed, induced Mrs Garcia to hand over my things to him. I lived with his family for some time, until fortunately I got another situation in the house of a German merchant.

Mrs Garcia I never saw again. She left Seville with her family shortly afterwards; and though I declined to have any steps taken to punish her, the story got about, and she was shunned even more than before. Where she went to I do not know, but those who hated her most whispered that it was to Santa Alba, whither Father Avila had been removed by his ecclesiastical superiors.

NOTE—As many of the people mentioned in this story are still alive, I have thought it better to alter the names throughout. In other respects I have told the story as it was told to me by the lady I have called Fräulein Schaller.

VI

A GHOSTLY
BURGLAR

I HAVE NEVER SEEN A GHOST, but I have heard one. At the time I was apprenticed to a firm of merchants, and on the evening of the ghostly visitation I was working late at the office alone, journalising and posting as hard as I could. Being book-keeper, I had a little room to myself, which was detached from the other parts of the office by a short flight of steps, at the top of which was a glass door directly facing the outer door of the office. There were no houses near, and I had ascertained on my return from dinner that the office above was locked, and would not be occupied that evening.

From about half-past seven until nearly eleven o'clock I had written on uninterrupted. I stood on a little platform making entries alternately in the journal and ledger, and was as merry as anyone could be who had refused an invitation to a dance, because he had work which must be attended to. I whistled an occasional tune, and all sorts of innumerable thoughts went through my head; not one of them, I am positive, having any bearing whatever on the awful agony I was so soon to endure.

Timid I have always been, but constant usage had quite hardened me to be the only occupant after dark of a large, dismal-looking office, which, with the gas burning low, looked sufficiently eerie, especially when a slow fire, with an occasional burst of flame, threw deep shadows behind desks and tables. The postman had long since made his deliveries, and I remember well how a year or two before this the thud of the letters in the box had startled me. Now that I had got accustomed to it, it made no impression upon me; and even the tap made on the window by some passing youths, when they saw the front room lighted, failed to rouse me even to see who the offenders were.

I was thoroughly engrossed in my work, when suddenly I heard someone carefully and cautiously turn the handle of the office door, and gently shut the door behind him. My first thought was one of wonder how he had passed through the outside door, for it had been shut, and only a Chubb key would open it. But I reflected that if he was a burglar he would find ways of doing that, and I was brought to face the question of what the object was that had brought him there at such a time. An uneasy sensation passed over me as I remembered that a large sum of money had been paid that day after bank hours, and that the bank-notes lay in the drawer of the safe. The man evidently knew that someone was in the office, for he opened and closed the door so quietly that, had I not been very sharp at hearing, I should probably not have caught the peculiar click the lock made in shutting. I fancied for a time that I must have been mistaken, for no other sound was discernible. My pen stopped, and I pricked up my ears to listen for the least indication of movement. The intruder was evidently afraid that he had startled me, because for about a minute he was perfectly still. I dared not move, but waited patiently to ascertain if there was actually a man, or if it was only my imagination befooling me. Would he never move? Neither of us made the slightest sound for about a minute. I expect it was only a minute, but it seemed an hour. I have known days go quicker than that awful minute.

And then I heard his footsteps—slowly, softly, gliding towards the safe. I hope never to go through the same intense agony of excitement as I then suffered. I could not move, I could not speak; my legs were fixed, my tongue was tied, my hands shook.

I distinctly felt each hair of my head rise and stand on end; my heart jumped and thumped so that I feared it would force its way through my ribs; and then a cold—deathly cold—shiver went right down my body. My feet were like lumps of ice. I put my hand to my brow and found it quite wet with perspiration. These sensations rapidly followed one another, all in the space of a very few seconds. I felt as though I should faint, but the mysterious sound of the light, cautious, wary footstep stopped, and I knew that the burglar was beside the safe. What a whirl of excited imaginations went through my mind! My masters would be robbed. I would be murdered! My fevered brain was not in a fit state to decide upon any course of action. Trembling from head to foot I stepped quietly to the glass door of my room, and looked down the steps into the large office. The door was shut, and the shadows cast by the fire were dancing up and down the walls like great gaunt, grizzly ghosts. Their ghastly shadows frightened me still more. What should I do? Cry out for help? No; for no help was near; the villain would rush on me, perhaps with a band of accomplices, and in my nervous condition I could not hope to withstand their attack, and would be a dead man in two minutes. Should I quietly slip out of the window of my room, which looked into a back street, and go for the police; or else try to forget the whole circumstance, and smother my conscience. No: for that would be cowardly; and before I could have summoned help the robber would be off with his plunder. To run away was my momentary decision; but when I considered that I would be held responsible, and when I got sufficiently clear-headed to think that in so doing I would be betraying my master's interests, the idea was dismissed. The only plan left was to face the villain. At the thought of this all my old trepidation returned, but I dared not give way again to my weakness; and so, without further delay, picked up the poker (what a miserable weapon I thought it compared with the revolvers and daggers I expected my enemy to possess!) opened the door of the room, and marched down the steps into the office. The safe was situated in a recess between the large office and the partner's room, so that I could not see my antagonist when I reached the office. How I wished he would take the offensive and do something! But he made no sound, no movement, and so I stamped loudly and shouted, "Who's there?" in a tone which indicated greater fright than I would wish to have shown.

No soldier ever went into battle with more craven feelings than mine. As I walked across the office, only a few yards, my mind was full of visions. I pictured my mother weeping over the gory corpse of her murdered boy; I read the account of the crime in the morrow's newspaper. All the good and the evil I had done were present to me, and I saw the faces of friends I had not seen for years; and alas, would now never see again in this life! Thus half-dreaming I approached the spot where I knew my enemy to be standing. I turned the corner, and with a determination not to be killed without a struggle I brought my weapon down with my utmost strength. It failed to strike him; and then expecting every moment to be my last, I looked up—and saw nobody.

I looked all around, searched the presses, peered under the desks, but could find no trace of anyone. I shut up the office, and went home to pass an almost sleepless night, in which the short time I was asleep was enlivened by the most desperate encounters with invisible burglars. In the morning I found that the office was as I had left it; no one but myself had been there, and the sounds of doors and footsteps had been an imagination.

I told what I had seen to my fellow-clerk and friend Robert Winton, and, as I half-expected, got from him no sympathy. He put it down to imagination; and so averse was he to admitting that there could be anything else in the affair, that he almost succeeded in convincing me. Certainly I thought very little about it afterwards.

Next week the Indian mails were heavy, and had given me a great deal of what I looked upon as extra work; and I found that, to have my books posted up, I must return that night to the office. When I got there, I must confess that the memory of my previous week's experience was strong in me, and it was some little time before I got fairly settled down to work. At last I did so, and had almost completed my task, about a quarter to eleven, when I heard the handle of the glass-door being touched. I turned round at once, saw nothing, stepped forward, and looked through—still nothing was to be seen; and had it not been through what I must confess to have been abject fear I should have opened the door and examined the office. But I could not do it. I went back to my books, and putting my head on my arms, tried to reason myself into courage. Again, in it may have been one minute, or it may have been ten, I do not know, the handle was moved. Look round I could not. The door opened, was shut, and the same footsteps I had heard before I heard now. On they went, they stopped at the safe. The safe! My fears were gone, or rather surmounted, by the feeling that I was responsible for its contents, for I had opened it to get out my books, and everything of value in it was exposed to a burglar. I forgot my previous week's experience, forgot everything but that the man should go, and go with nothing stolen.

I picked up my rule and prepared to start, when the slightness of my weapon made me think of the poker, and that, of last week. What was I to do? For a moment I thought, then moved on. If it was only imagination no harm was done; if there was a man there, I must protect my master's property. Slowly I crept towards the corner round which stood the safe, prepared the poker, then round with a rush, and a downward blow with all my strength. God! I struck something; for there was a groan, a flash of light, and a heavy fall. Wild with the shock and fear, which now came back upon me with redoubled force, I shouted for help.

I came to myself to find Bob Winton sponging my face, and a policeman standing behind him. I had fainted, and, without being allowed to speak, I was taken home.

Some days afterwards when I was better, I heard what had happened.

Bob Winton had resolved on a practical joke at my expense, and getting the duplicate key of the office, had slipped in at eleven, and came along to the glass door. He was surprised to find me absent from my desk, though the books lay there, and had just opened the door when he heard a heavy fall, and then my cries for help. He rushed in, caught me as I fell, and found a man lying on the floor in front of the safe, his head cut and bleeding, and a dark lantern, with false keys and burglars' tools on the floor beside him. Laying me down on the floor he rushed to the street, and was fortunate enough to see a policeman on the other side a little way off. He called him over and brought him in.

The burglar, who was only stunned by my blow, was removed to the police-office. He was known to the police, and his trial resulted in his being sentenced to ten years' penal servitude. I have never worked at night alone in the office since. I do not want to encounter any more such visitors, even though they give me a week's notice of their arrival.

VII

THE GHOST'S
LETTER

I DO NOT BY ANY MEANS vouch for the truth of the following story in all its details, but simply submit it as I got it from the lips of one who evidently gave it full credence. It was told me by the side of a smithy fire, the lurid and fitful glare of which added not a little to the eerie feeling the story was, under any circumstances, calculated to inspire. I endeavoured to get from my informant some idea of the period when the principal events occurred, but in this I was altogether unsuccessful. He admitted that it all happened before his time, but further averred that "they were neither deid nor sick that had gude eneuch mind aboot it; although," he added, "there's nane o' them hereawa' noo that I ken o', binna auld John Dickson up-by at the plantin' side, an' he wad never speak o't ava when he could help it; nor will he speak o't to this day, for I hae tried him mair than yince mysel', an' gat nocht but a moothfu' o' soot for my pains."

Having no particular desire for such an experience, whether literally or metaphorically, I forbore prosecuting any further investigation of the affair than that afforded by the second-hand statements here reproduced. It may also be mentioned that the narrative is given in the phraseology of the person who favoured me with it; or, at least, in as near an approach to it as my memory now enables me to furnish. His dialect was the rich, broad Doric of the south-west of Scotland.

Having asked me if I knew a small house about a mile and a quarter to the northward of where we then were, and situated a short distance from the highway on the left-hand side, he began—

"There was a gey queer thing happened in that same hoose, yince on a time. There was a *gaun-man* —that's a packman body, ye ken—that was makin' his way alang the road, yae awesome stormy winter nicht. He was wadin' amaist knee-deep in the snaw, an' fan' that it was hopeless to attemp' gettin' the len'th o' the clachan here, that he was boun' for, an' whaur he had ettled to spen' the nicht. He was like to gie up a'thegither an' lie doon, but had that muckle gumption to ken that gin he did gie way to his weariedness, it was ten to yin he wad fa' asleep, an' if he did that he wad very likely never wauken in this warl'. Sae on he trudged as best he could, aye takin' a bit glance owre his shouther on baith sides o' the road, to see if he couldna get a glisk o' some winnock-licht to direct him—

To whaur a shelter micht be got,
In fu'some ha' or lamely cot.

"At lang an' len'th, as luck wad hae't, he saw a bit glimmer comin' frae the airt o' the hoose that I spak o'. Sae owre the dyke he loupit, an' made his way to whaur the licht was seen. He knockit at the door, an' a voce through the keyhole cried, 'Wha's there at sic an untimeous 'oor o' the nicht?' 'A puir traveller wha has tint his gate amang the snaw, an' is that sair dune he can gang nae farder, tho' he should lie doon an' dee at your threshol'.' Wi' that the door was opened, an' the sair, forfouchen creatur' was inveeted to come in an' stop a' nicht. Weel, in he gaed, after shakin' the waucht o' snaw aff his duds an' his pack in the passage. The gudewife saw by his face he was a decent chiel, sae she made him a bit cup o' tea afore he gaed to his bed. Then she put on a bit fire in his bedroom, an' hung his o'ercoat in front o' the kitchen ingle, an laid his soakit shoon on the hob, as he had been her ain son.

"After he was ben, he sat doon to toast his feet afore he wad strip himsel', for, as I hae said, it was an unco cauld searchin' nicht. He aye carried a gude fu' wallet wi' him, an' he took it into the bedroom, altho' he had nae intention o' regalin' himsel' ony mair for that nicht, for he had been weel eneuch enterteened in the kitchen. But there's many a thing that folk does mair as a matter o' habit than onything else, an' I believe it was just use an' wont that made him tak' his wallet ben the hoose wi' him. (Hoo-ever, it's but little to the purpose what put it in his heid to do sae.) Weel, when he had het his shins a wee bit, he gat up to his feet to throw aff his claes, when a feelin' that he couldna account for cam' owre him—a feeling that there was surely some ither *presence* in the apairtment forbye his ain. It wasna that he either saw or heard onything at this time; but, somehoo or ither, he was convinced in his ain min' that he wasna a'thegither his leefu' lane. He lookit an' he listened, but a' to nae purpose. He opened a press that stude wi' its back to the wa', an' keekit ablow the bed, but nocht was to be seen, either in the shape o' a human bein', or *what had ever been yin*. An' yet, as I was tellin' ye, he was nearly as certain as that the breath was in his ain body that he had company in the room o' yae kin' or anither.

"As ye may wewl suppose, he grew geyan nervous an' uneasy, an' tried hard to persuade himsel' that his fear was only the effec' o' his exposure to the blast. Hooanever, he couldna get rid o' the notion; sac instead o' takin' aff his claes, he sat doon again at the fireside, to see if he could compose his min' a kennin' afore he gaed to his bed.

"He hadna been mony meenits sitten doon, when a sort o' glamour filled the room frae the tae en' to the tither; while, at the same time, the lowe o' the caunle on the mantelpiece, an' the fire in the grate, baith brunt as blue as the cludless lift on a simmer mornin'. Gif he was donnert-ways afore, he was ten times waur noo, for he kent there was nae langer ony doot, but that something uncanny was aboot to tak' place. He was sae muckle terrified he could neither steer nor scraigh for help. Sae there he sat as muveless as a milestane on the road to Girvan, an' if he wasna in an unco like plicht my name's no Tammas McBryde, an' this is no' Wullie Renton's smiddy.

"The unyirthly mist (or whatever it was) grew gradually thicker an' thicker. Then he saw the dim ootline o' a man's shape sittin' wi' a quill pen in its haun' an' a sheet o' writin' paper lyin' on the corner o' a table that its elbow was restin' on.

"The packman glowered at the apparition, an' the apparition glowered back at the packman, but neither o' them spak' for a while at first.

"At last, the puir, dazed body opened his wallet, an' took oot a daud o' ait-meal cake an' a lump o' cheese, an' raiket them ower to the figure fornent him. But the ghaist shook its heid. Then he drew oot a flask wi' a drap o' whusky in it, and handed that owre. But again the ghaist shook its heid. Neist he lichtit his pipe an' held it oot in gude-gaun order. But, for the third time, the ghaist shook its heid.

"'Weel, weel, neibour,' quo' the packman, 'e'en as ye like'—for by that time his terror began to grow less an' his power o' utterance to come back—'but gin ye're determined no' to partake o' my cheer, for ony sake tell me what's the natur' o' your mission to this hoose, or for what purpose ye hae honoured me wi' your company.'

"Wi' that the ghaist took its pen an' began to scribble on the sheet o' paper that lay on the table. When it had finished, it handed the manuscript to the packman. An' this was what it wrote, as near as I can min'. (I needna' forget it, for its been tauld me mair than yince by them that kent weel aboot it.)

'I was murdered mony a lang year since in this vera room. It was dune by a man that had a pair o' neibourless een in his heid. My mortal remains lie aneath the hearthstane at your feet. The murderer took my hat, an' threw it into the Milltown loch, to mak' it appear I had been drooned there. Fare ye weel, frien', for I hae nae mair to add, only that my name was Andrew Hyslop.'

At this stage of the recital, I took the liberty of interposing a few questions. Amongst others, I enquired if the phantom had ever been known to visit the dwelling before. Of this my friend was rather uncertain, but seemed satisfied that, at all events, it had never before ventured on any revelations. My next query was, what became of the document thus placed in the pedlar's hands under such extraordinary circumstances? My informant's version of that was, that the writing had entirely vanished on the advent of a new day, although it had been perfectly legible for a short time after the exit of the shady visitant who had penned it.

On expressing myself as so far satisfied on these points, the narrator was encouraged to proceed.

"As sune as the spectre had raiket the packman the sheet o' paper, it gaed clean oot o' sicht like a clap o' your haun'. At the same moment, the haze cleared awa' as it never had been, while the flame o' the ingle an' the licht o' the caunle changed to their ain colours. The packman spelled oot the writin' till he was fairly maister o't, for I believe he was nae great scholar ony mair than mysel'. Then he slippit the paper in his pocket, an' gaed awa' to his bed as gin nocht had happened to disturb him. Weel-I-wat, he had a stoot heart for a' the fley he had got, to stap a message frae the ither warl' in his pooch; but it's wonnerfu' what folk can do when they're pitten til't, an' he was anxious to preserve the pruif o' the ghaist's presence, if he was spared to tell what he had seen an' learned that nicht.

"Neist mornin', he tauld the folk o' the hoose the haill story as I hae tauld it to you. They were a wee chary aboot takin' it in, sae he whuppit the sheet o' paper oot o' his pocket to convince them it was nae histor' o' lees or nonsense he was rammin' doon their throats. But, whatever was the explanation o't, there was nae mair writin' on the sheet than there is on the breist o' your shirt this present meenit. They lauched at the puir chiel, an' said he had only dreamed the haill business; an' mair an' farder, that the sheet o' paper was the same yin that had been left on the table the day afore by the dochter o' the hoose, wha had been scribblin' twa or three lines to her lad—an' nae faut. But he insisted that he had been as wide waukin' as ever he had been in his life; sae to show him, as they thocht, that it was naething but a megrim, they gat the hearthstane lifted. An' ye may guess their surprise an' horror in daein' sae—for there, sure eneuch, was the skeleton o' a human bein'!

"There was a fine hoo-d'ye-dae through the kintraside when the story gat wing, for everybody thocht the by-gane tenant o' the place had ackwally been drooned in the Milltown loch. He had been an auld meeser o' a body wha leeved his lane, an' there was routh o' odd cash foun' in stockin' legs an' sic like after his death; but, as he had kept it in sae mony different neuks an' orra places o' yae sort an' anither, the authorities—for he had nae relations hereaboots—couldna discover hoo muckle he was worth, or whether his goods an' gear were a' there or no', when they took possession o' the preemises. It was a nine day's wouner, like mony anither concern we hae seen; an' after that, naebody fashed his thoom aboot him or his belangin's, when he was awa'.

"Among ithers wha cam' to look at the skeleton, was yin—Doctor Lowrie; an' after he had examined it, he said the man had dootless come to his death by foul play. He was a gey gleg, lang-heided chap, Dr Lowrie, an' nae mistak'. We had nane to match him in this pairt o' the kintra sin' he de'ed, an' there was jist as few like him when he was leevin'. Ay, weel, he kent by a ding in the skull that the man had got an unco sair crack on the croon wi' some weapon. But, mair an' farder, he gied his opeenion, that the blow had been dealt wi' a *left haun'*. Hoo he arrived at sic a conclusion is fairly ayont my comprehension, but sae he made it oot it had been dune, an' it's mair than likely sae it was, for, as I said afore, there was few things could cheat Dr Lowrie.

"The remains was lifted an' buried decently in the kirkyard, an' nac mair was ever made o' the mystery frae that day to this. Mony a body was on the ootlook when strangers cam' aboot the distric', but nane could ever come across *a left-haundit man wi' a pair o' neibourless een in his heid*.

"Sae that's a' the story, as I hae aften heard it tauld when I was a younker, an' I firmly believe it's every word true, only ye're at perfect leeberty to form your ain judgment aboot it."

When he had finished, I put a few more questions bearing on the authenticity of his tale, such as how it came that the only individual in the vicinity who was old enough to remember it was so reticent, and even uncivil, when the subject was mentioned; and whether the said individual believed as implicitly in the truth of my friend's averments as he did himself? He replied to the effect that the gentleman in question had no doubt whatever about the finding of the skeleton beneath the hearth, for he was one of the few privileged parties who had seen it at the time. "But," he continued, "he's yin o' the sceptical kin' anent the packman's share in the business o' the discovery, an' declares that the banes were foun' by accident; an' that the report aboot the ghaist wasna circulated till after-hin'. Hooever, it's nae manner o' use to argue wi' thrawn customers like auld John Dickson, for—preserve us a'!—it's surely plain eneuch to ony unprejudiced pairty that if the ghaist o' the murdered man hadna let somebody ken whaur his banes were hid they wad been lyin' there yet."

I confess that I was not quite so satisfied of the conclusiveness of my informant's closing deduction as he seemed to be himself, but did not then demur, as otherwise I should have laid myself open to the charge of casting doubts on what he had been so careful to particularise for my instruction in ghostly lore.

In connection with the foregoing legend—for most people in these philosophical days of ours will be disposed to regard it as little else—I may be pardoned for referring to a rather striking coincidence which came under my own observation. It may at the same time be stated that, but for the coincidence alluded to, I should very probably never have thought of giving the story publicity at all.

A considerable time after the date when I heard the story beside the smithy fire, and in a totally different part of the country, I chanced to be in a place of business making some purchases. As the goods were intended for transmission to a distance, I asked the shopkeeper to pack them well for me in a small box, which he did. On going to the hotel where I was staying I opened the box to have another look at the articles before sending them away. I found, in unpacking them, that the vacant spaces in the box were filled with pieces of waste paper of various kinds. One of these pieces, which was evidently a fragment of an old newspaper, arrested my attention on account of its soiled appearance. On opening and smoothing it out, my interest and amazement may be imagined, as my eye rested on the following portion of a paragraph, of which, unfortunately for the gratification of my curiosity, the rest had been torn away.

The wretched culprit also confessed to the chaplain of the prison, on the night before his execution, that he had been guilty of a previous robbery and murder somewhere in the south of Scotland. He had, it seems, some physical peculiarities which were rather noticeable. It was chiefly his *left hand* that he employed in whatever he did, even to the signing of his name; while *his eyes*, strange to say, *were of a distinctly different colour from each other—one being of a cold grey, and the other of a ——*

The remainder was wanting.

There were other items of what had once been news on the scrap, but nothing by which either the name of the journal, its date of issue, or place of publication, could be ascertained. So there the matter stands.

VIIII

HELEN, UNRESTFUL HELEN

THE WESTMORELANDS were spending the summer in the vicinity of a popular resort. "By good fortune," Jack wrote, "we have procured a roomy old mansion, with spacious grounds; and your presence alone was necessary to complete our pleasure."

Having accepted the invitation, I shortly found myself one of a gay company enjoying the Westmorelands' hospitality. The advantages of Fern Chase had not been over-rated: it was the residence of a family then abroad, the only stipulation of the owner in letting it being that some rooms in a wing adjoining should be occupied by his eldest son, who remained at home. We often saw him passing to and from his rooms, and though we regarded him with great interest, he seemed oblivious of our presence.

George Dare was a strikingly handsome man, despite his great dark eyes, wearing an expression of melancholy, which pervaded indeed his whole bearing. Louise Westmoreland and I often wondered if he were weighted with some secret sorrow, or if he were only a dreamer. And by the way, to be candid, love of pretty Louise was the real object of my visit to her brother; but I was provoked to find a rival in Tracy Gordon —a careless, gay, good-hearted fellow.

Louise, winsome fairy, was a trifle coquettish, and through this trait in her, innocent as May zephyrs, I was to learn the hidden history of George Dare.

One evening Louise exclaimed, laughingly, "Who will accept a dare, *mes cavaliers*? My maid has discovered a key of the apartments of the man of mystery. Papa and mamma won't know it, and it will be such fun."

Forgetting impropriety in Louise's witchery, Gordon and I eagerly volunteered to do her will. Mischievously she tossed the key towards us. We sprang forward, but I first caught it. All was darkness, when I found the entrance to the wing. Inserting the key, I easily admitted myself. The first room was in darkness, but in one beyond burned a dim lamp; hastily reaching it, I raised it. A feeling of undefined terror had possessed me since my entrance. The room was evidently the study of a cultured person; book-cases lined the walls, and about were paintings and statuary. On a desk beside an open book was a cluster of crumbling roses, tied with faded creamy ribbon. Over everything lay the dust of years. But in the strangeness of one object I forgot all else. It was the life-size portrait of a woman—young and exquisitely beautiful. The graceful form was clad in creamy satin, creamy roses nestling amidst frosty lace, and resting in the meshes of golden hair. Some she held loosely with one hand, the other was extended in an attitude of entreaty. This strange posture, and gleaming pallor of skin, added to the deep unrest of the violet eyes, seemed weird and unearthly. Earth-costumed though she was, did ever living woman wear that rapt, awful expression?

Rising to examine more closely, I became conscious of a presence in the room. I heard the rustle of a dress, felt a hand laid lightly on my shoulder, and turned to behold beside me a woman. Merciful Heaven! the same queenly woman whose portrait was before me, attired in the very costume, standing in the very same supplicating attitude, her yearning eyes gazing into mine.

I endeavoured to command speech, but something in the cold, statuesque form froze every faculty. A feeling of numbness overcame me. I fell to the ground. When consciousness returned, the light had grown dim, and the mysterious woman had disappeared. I longed for air and companionship. Gathering strength, I fled from the rooms and soon reached my friends.

They were waiting anxiously.

"Tell us of your visit," they cried, seeing my excited appearance.

Only Louise whispered, softly, "Has anything happened? Are you ill?"

"Have you encountered a real ghost?" laughed my rival.

This roused me. I told all. A burst of merriment followed.

"Why, old fellow!" said Jack, "you fell asleep gazing at the picture. You ate a hearty dinner, took no exercise, and slumbered. *Voilà tout.*"

My anger rose when Tracy whispered to Louise, "By Jove! too much champagne gives a fellow odd fancies sometimes." Then aloud, "Better limit yourself to one glass hereafter, my dear boy."

I grew irate, vehemently protesting the truth of my story, declaring, with a witness, I would return to the apartments the following night. This proved satisfactory, and the subject dropped. The succeeding night, accompanied by the party, I sought the wing. Jack proposed my entering alone, they being in proximity if anything unusual occurred.

Encouraged by the knowledge of their nearness, I entered the study, and with eyes fastened on the *portière* awaited the development of events. I had not long to wait.

Soon a small white hand raised the *portière*, disclosing the beautiful vision of the preceding evening. She slowly advanced. Pausing before me, and laying one hand on my shoulder, she stood in an attitude of entreaty as before.

Repressing the shudder her touch inspired, I exclaimed, "In the name of God, who are you?"

Slowly the answer, *"Helen, unrestful Helen."*

Turning with quickened steps she disappeared through the *portière*. Hastily following, I found the adjoining room unoccupied; she must have sought the outer door. I laid one hand on the knob. Simultaneously it turned from the outside, and I was face to face with George Dare.

Confusion drowned all other feelings. I waited a rebuke for my intrusion in his apartments. Instead he said, quietly,

"Follow me, I have something to say to you."

Reaching the study with returned composure, I explained the reason of my intrusion, and begged pardon for the offence. This he gave with rare sweetness; then he said, gravely,

"You have seen her?"

I bowed my head, affirmatively.

"Do you know what you have seen?"

"No," I answered.

"You beheld no living woman, but an apparition."

I had already felt it.

He continued—

"You and I alone have seen this vision. I will tell the story, but on a promise it shall be sacred with you until I die. Heretofore I have guarded alone the secret of my wretched, exiled life. Always reserved, devoted to study, I cared little for society in general—less for that of women—until Helen came to visit my sister. From the moment I beheld her I loved her with the intensity of my silent nature. I left seclusion, and was beside her constantly. I cared for nothing, thought of nothing, but her; and my rapture was boundless when she told me my love was returned. We lived in Paradise. Alas! the serpent was not long in entering. Helen withdrew from all admirers, yielding to my exactions; for I was wildly jealous of any one approaching her. My brother Archie professed open admiration for her, and I hated him.

"One day, hearing her voice, I entered the drawing-room. Bending over her, whilst she sang, was Archie. I stood, burning with rage, watching them unseen until Archie was called away. Standing before Helen, I cruelly reproached her, and, despite her tearful protestations, I angrily left the room.

"That evening I remained sullenly in my study, determining not to attend a ball given at our house. 'Helen might enjoy Archie's company undisturbed,' I said, bitterly.

"About eleven o'clock she came for me, looking radiantly beautiful, and besought me to come with her as I had promised. Placing before me the flowers you see in ashes she stood in the attitude portrayed in her picture. A demon possessed me. Hearing every gentle word, noting every pleading gesture, I sat without raising my head. A moment of noting silence, then I was alone—alone with the roses she had left—sending their fragrance into my heart. Their mission was fulfilled—anger and jealousy fled.

"Filled with contrition, I entered the ball-room to beg forgiveness. Helen was not there, so I sought the conservatory, full of repentance and love. Yes, she was there; and beside her was Archie, declaring ardently his passion. I noted not the withdrawal of her hand from his, of the unhappy gravity of her countenance. They have since risen like avenging phantoms.

"Unseen, in a fury of rage, I rushed from the spot.

"Leaving father a hasty note, pleading a sudden business call, I fled from the house. In a few weeks my eyes were opened by a letter from Archie, saying Helen had refused his love, and reproaching me bitterly for injustice to her, whose love, he protested, was greater than mine. She had been ill, and was then abroad for her health.

"I wrote to her words of penitent love, in which my very soul went forth, beseeching to be allowed to go to her. This letter she never received, and no reply coming I thought my jealousy had destroyed my attachment. One day I learned she had returned to this country, and was failing rapidly. That night I was in this study preparing for my departure to Helen the following day, when, to my infinite surprise, I felt a light hand laid on my shoulder, and turning beheld her beside me.

"With a joyful cry I was about to enfold her in my arms—but, O Heaven! that awful pallor, those yearning eyes, were not of life. I knew then my darling was no longer of earth.

"Every night at the hour in which I saw her last, she comes apparelled as on that fateful eve. And standing as she did—then entreatingly—here in the room in which her heart was broken, is my beautiful love, condemning me to expiate, by earthly visits, the sin of her too deep love. All I can do now is to share her penance. The picture I myself painted from the apparition."

Dare sighed heavily. I rose to go. Grasping my hand, he bade me farewell for ever.

When I returned to the house, they told me that, seeing the dark stranger coming, they had basely fled, leaving me to my fate—anticipating "my utter annihilation."

"Was it a woman, ghost, or champagne?" cried Tracy.

My promise rose vividly, and I answered "champagne."

Years passed, and I faithfully kept the secret, even from my wife, Louise; but, chancing near Fern Chase, I heard of George Dare's death, and that again the family were abroad. Bribing a servant to allow me to enter the haunted wing, provided with a lamp, I awaited the apparition.

Eleven, twelve, one o'clock passed, with nothing to disturb the silence. Three consecutive nights I devoted to ascertaining if Helen still returned; and when the third night passed without seeing her I knew that poor George Dare and his unhappy love were done with earthly unrest, and prayed Heaven that they were united in eternal happiness.

IX

THE 31st OF DECEMBER

I, WALTER RUDGE, considered myself very lucky when it was finally settled that I was to go as tutor to Mr Graverston's grandson, at Naughton Towers. To the youngest son of a poor clergyman £75 a year seemed untold riches, and one bleak, cold day in November I left my home in Scotland, and started on my journey to Naughton with a light heart. About' five o'clock in the afternoon I left the express at D—— Junction, feeling, I must confess, rather depressed. My high spirits had all vanished, and the local train felt very slow and tedious after the express. The third-class carriage was swimming with the drippings from many umbrellas, for it had been raining heavily all the later part of the day. At last the train slowly steamed into Barnon Station, where I had to alight, my railway journey being there at an end. It seemed a miserable little place, where one man appeared to undertake all the duties of stationmaster, ticket collector, and porter. While engaged getting my luggage out of the van I felt a slight tap on my shoulder, and a hoarse voice said in my ear, "Be you the gent for the Towers?"

I turned round and saw a wizened old man standing behind me. He had on an antiquated coachman's coat, with many capes, much too large for him; his bent legs were encased in leggings which showed off their thinness; and his head was adorned with a hat which seemed coeval with himself.

"Yes; I am the gentleman for the Towers," I replied, in answer to his question; and then added, "I suppose you are Mr Graverston's coachman?"

He only glared at me as he shouldered my box and led the way out of the station, where a broken-down looking gig stood waiting. The old man got in, having first stowed away my box at the back, and I silently followed his example. After much jerking at the reins, the animal, which by courtesy only could be called a horse, at last moved off, and we rolled slowly along the road. The night was very dark, and the rain fell in torrents.

"Have we far to go?" I said at last, by way of beginning a conversation with my taciturn companion; "we seem to have gone about two miles."

"Ah! a good bit," he replied. "Mebbe three miles more."

"Indeed! Then the nearest village and station are at Barnon. Naughton Towers must be quite away in the country. It will be lonely enough in winter."

"Ah!" he said; and I could tell by his voice that he had turned his head suddenly in my direction. "Lonely at all times; a d—d lonely place."

Feeling rather surprised by the warmth of this reply, I determined to ask no more questions, so we jolted on in silence for about an hour, when the horse seemed to stop of his own accord before a gate in a wood. The old man got down to open it, and I could see that we turned into a private avenue. After going up this for half-a-mile the huge outline of a house was dimly seen in the darkness. We pulled up at the door, and I jumped down, glad to stretch my legs, cramped with so much sitting. My coachman got down too, and after some trouble unearthed my box from the back; then, to my surprise, he remounted his gig, and prepared to drive away.

"Why," I cried, "where are you off to; and who am I to get to carry my box in; don't you live here?"

"Live here! no, not likely," he replied. "I'm Farmer Stubbs's man, and the old 'un hired me to-day to drive ye over. Ah! he's a queer 'un, he his; I advise you to take care of him and keep out of his way."

I had been a month at Naughton Towers as tutor, and would have given all my worldly goods (alas, how few they were!) for a good excuse to leave the place.

Mr Graverston, my master, had mentioned to me in his letters that his grandson was backward and dull, but I found that he really was intellectually weak, and this was a great disappointment to me. He was a sickly boy of eleven, and very small for his age; but it was Mr

Graverston himself who puzzled me most. He seemed to hate the poor child so; and I often saw him look at him with a glance that froze my very blood—it seemed to express so much hatred. Naturally the boy hated his grandfather in return; and once when I asked him the reason of it, he cried out, "Oh, the 31st of December—the 31st of December—if only I could remember what he did then in the east room, long, long——."

His look and voice alarmed me much, and I never mentioned the subject again, for I felt sure that all excitement was bad for him.

The most rigid economy was practised in the house; the only servants being an old woman and her husband, the latter devoting most of his time to the gardens, and thus leaving most of the household work to his wife. The house was a damp, gloomy, old place, most of the rooms being unfurnished, and the east room, to which my pupil had referred so wildly, was a large room at the very top of the house, quite empty, except for a table and some rickety old chairs, which stood at one end; it was so gloomy that one visit was sufficient for me, and I was glad to come down again to the more cheerful parts of the house.

I longed for a companion of my own age to relieve the monotony of my life, and to whom I could have confided my fears concerning Mr Graverston's sanity; but such longings were hopeless, for the house stood alone in those solitary woods, the nearest labourer's cottage being nearly a mile away, and the only village within reach was that of Barnon, which was fully eight miles distant.

One evening as George, my pupil, was not feeling well, I sent him to bed early; he had been unnaturally flushed and excited all day, and towards the evening grew so much worse that I felt quite alarmed about him. I determined not to go to bed till very late, so that if he did not seem better I might alarm his grandfather, and have a doctor sent for.

I sat reading for several hours in the study, and was just thinking of going to have another look at George, and then turning into bed myself, when I was startled by a sound at the other end of the room and, looking round, I saw Mr Graverston entering the door. His appearance startled me; his eyes seemed starting from their sockets, and an unnatural restlessness seemed to make it impossible for him to keep still an instant.

"Ah, Rudge," he cried, "you here? You are late to-night; but perhaps, like me, you are sitting up to see the first of New Year?"

(I suddenly remembered it was the 31st of December.)

"Suppose, as we are both wakeful, we sit up together."

To sit up with him, when he was in that excited state, was the last thing I wished to do; but I know not what made me reply, "Certainly, sir! I am not at all sleepy; and shall be very glad to sit up with you. We have not long to wait for the New Year. It is already a quarter past eleven."

"Come with me," he said, suddenly laying his hand, which felt like ice, on mine; "come up and sit in my room! Ha! ha! they may say what they like, but though it is the 31st December what do I care."

His laugh froze my blood; it seemed to me the shriek of a maniac, but I dared not disobey him, for he was a strong, powerfully-built old man, and I noticed that he carried in his hand a heavy iron ruler. Silently he led me up the stairs, and along the dark passages till we reached the east room, entered it, and found a lighted tallow candle guttering on the table, making a feeble ray of light in the shadowy darkness of the room. I sat down on one of the chairs feeling (shall I be very much despised for the confession?) horribly frightened. The man was a maniac—of that I was convinced—and I felt that any attempt on my part to leave him would bring down his fury on my head. Suddenly he stopped walking, and turned round facing me.

"Well, Rudge!" he cried, "how do you like spending an hour or two up here with me in my favourite room; you sit shivering there on your chair, looking as if you had seen a ghost. You young men of to-day have not half the pluck of us old ones. Why, in this very room, four years ago, with my own hands, I killed my daughter-in-law. The thing was quite easily done; she offended me with her ceaseless cries of, 'Do this, do that, all for the boy's sake,' and so on; and so one day I got her up here and caught her by the neck; one squeeze in the right place—so" (he made a horrible sound in his throat), "and the deed was done. Can I ever forget her yell as I caught her, or that voice which still seems to say in my ear—'The 31st of December!'"

I sat rooted to my chair in horror. Graverston came quite close to me, and whispered in my ear,

"Come and I will show you where I put the body; it never was discovered—look here."

He opened a long, narrow door, at one side of the fireplace, and beckoned me to come and look in, but I could not for my life have moved from the spot where I sat. At that moment the clock from the stables struck out twelve, loud and clear, and at the same time Mr Graverston uttered an unearthly scream. I looked at him, and saw that his face, which had been very much flushed before, had turned an awful, corpse-like whiteness; he was staring with starting eyeballs at the opposite end of the room.

"O heavens!" he shrieked in a voice of terror; "there she is; she has come for me." I started from my chair and saw the form of a woman slowly advancing towards us. She was dressed in ordinary attire, her dress seemed to have been pulled open at the throat, and showed some livid marks about her neck. She glided past me towards

Graverston, and I could see the expression of malignant hatred on her face. Just then the candle died down in its socket, and the room was left in total darkness. I could stand it no longer, and rushed from the fatal chamber.

How I managed to reach my own room I cannot tell, but I sat there till daylight, and then once again I directed my steps towards the east room. With a trembling hand I pushed open the door, and entered. The room had its usual gloomy appearance, but one of the chairs had been knocked over, and the cloth was pulled half off the table.

With a sickening feeling I went round to the other side of the table, and there, lying half-concealed by it, I found the body of John Graverston. His arms were thrown up above his head, as if to ward off some foe; but the look on his face I can never forget—it seemed to express such awful fear; the front of his shirt was open, and round his neck I saw the same dreadful marks which I had seen the night before on the woman. He had been strangled.

Of the horrors of the inquest and the following days I cannot speak. I at last got away from the fatal place, taking my pupil with me, for his guardians had intrusted him to my care, with a salary and allowances on the most generous scale. I travelled with him for some years, and when, through these same guardians' influence, I was appointed to the post which I now hold, he was so much stronger, mentally and physically, that he was relieved from any successor to me being appointed. He recurred, though very seldom, to his life at Naughton Towers, but never gave, even if he could, any explanation of his fear or of his wild sayings; and the curious part of it all is that inquiries which I made satisfied me that his mother had died in London of typhoid fever early in the month of May. What the cause of old Mr Graverston's hallucination—if it was only hallucination—was, I could not find out, nor whose were the bones which were found in the press he showed me on that awful night.

On winding up the affairs of John Graverston, some extraordinary papers were found in his desk, headed, "My Confessions," but they were written in such a rambling and incoherent fashion that nothing could be made of them. The house was sold as soon as possible, and as it was in such bad repair brought an absurdly low price. The present owner pulled the old building down; and in its place built a new and commodious house; and Naughton Towers, as I knew it, exists no longer.